COLD CUTS

By Steve Brewer

Cover design by Kelly Brewer

ISBN-13: 978-1987759648

ISBN-10: 1987759648

Chapter 1

"Baloney!" blurted Lucky Flanagan.

"*Bolonía*," Freddie Garcia gently corrected. "Bologna made in Mexico."

"No, I meant *baloney*, like, bullshit," Lucky said. "There's no way people will pay more for bologna than they will for steak."

"But Mexican bologna is illegal in the United States," Garcia said. "That makes it special and rare. Customers who grew up near the border get nostalgic for the bologna of their childhood."

Nostalgia seemed to be what they were selling at the old-fashioned butcher shop as well. The tall windows of Garcia's office looked out into the work space of *El Matador Carnicería*, where three stout brown men in blood-spattered white aprons hacked away at hunks of beef and pork. Another butcher wore white rubber gloves as he stuffed a long sausage wrapper with pink mush. The work area was thirty feet by twenty feet, crowded with a dozen steel tables that could be rolled from cooler to cutter to customer.

Beyond the butchers stood the sales counter with its neat displays of meats and, nearest the front entrance, a grocery area with shelves full of south-of-the-border delicacies. One white wall bore a faded mural of a poised matador getting the better of a weary-looking bull. The shop was brightly lit, mostly from sunlight pouring through windows that wrapped around the brick building.

Garcia might've worked his way up to the corner office, but he still looked like a butcher, with broad shoulders and strong hands. His forearms were muscular where the sleeves of his blue cowboy shirt cuffed back. A silver bolo tie cinched his collar around his thick neck. Garcia wore his black hair slicked straight back. He looked to be in his late forties, but there was no sign of gray in his hair or in his neatly trimmed mustache.

"I've lived in Albuquerque all my life," Lucky said. "How come I've never heard of this Mexican bologna?"

Garcia shrugged. "In some circles, it's well-known. Especially the Rojo brand, which comes in a red wrapper."

He held his hands about two feet apart, to indicate the size of the roll. Lucky had seen similar rolls behind glass at the sales counter.

"You've got regular old American bologna out there."

"Yes," Garcia said, "and that's fine for most customers. But American bologna is pretty bland compared to Rojo, which has little bits of fat and dark meat in it. You cut a slice, and the cross-section looks like summer sausage or salami."

"Why is it illegal?"

"They process it differently down in Mexico. Doesn't pass our government regulations."

"But people want to eat it anyway."

"Some people do."

"And they'll pay premium prices to get it?"

"Farther away from the border you go, the more expensive it gets. You can buy a ten-pound roll in Juarez for six bucks and sell it in Denver for sixty."

"And here in Albuquerque?"

"Depends on the market. It's hot right now."

"Because people think it's exotic."

Garcia shrugged again, as if he couldn't explain why customers want what they want.

Lucky leaned back and crossed his long legs. He wore his usual black T-shirt and tight black jeans, and he was only now beginning to cool off, seated directly under Garcia's rattling air conditioner. Outside, heat waves shimmered over the asphalt parking lot. End of June in Albuquerque, hottest week of the year. Hot enough to make a man question his fashion choices.

"Round numbers," Lucky said. "Maybe you clear forty dollars a roll after you pay for your gas. If you're gonna bother to smuggle something across the border, why not something that really pays?"

"You mean drugs?" Garcia said. "Guns?"

Lucky's turn to shrug.

"You get caught bringing coke or guns across the border, you're looking at ten, fifteen years behind bars," Garcia said. "But Mexican bologna? It's a violation of USDA regulations. They confiscate the bologna, fine you a thousand bucks and let you go."

"No jail time?"

"Never. I think judges would feel silly, sending somebody to jail over sandwich meat."

That sounded right to Lucky. The whole thing seemed goofy, smuggling bologna. Even the courts wouldn't take it seriously.

"So where do I come in?" he said. "You call me up out of the blue, wake me up on a Monday morning, and ask me to come here. I don't know you. I don't know anything about Mexican bologna. How did you even get my number?"

"My boss met you somewhere." Garcia smiled. "Said you were the whitest motherfucker he'd ever seen. I have to say he's right. You look like that redheaded guy on late-night TV."

Lucky frowned. He'd heard the comparison before. One skinny redhead makes it big on talk-show television, and the others never hear the end of it.

"I thought *you* were the boss."

"Here at the butcher shop, I run things. But I've got a boss. Everybody's got a boss."

"Not me," Lucky said. "I'm strictly freelance."

Garcia let that go by without comment, but Lucky could tell from his expression that he heard "freelance" as "unemployed."

"So, where's the big boss?"

"The guy who owns the shop doesn't *work* here," Garcia said. "He owns lots of other businesses, too."

"Who is he?"

Garcia shook his head. "You don't need to know anything about him. You'll be dealing with me."

"Where did he see me?"

"Who knows? Who cares? You interested or not?"

"In smuggling bologna?"

"The border cops would never expect a gringo like you to smuggle Rojo into the country. You pick up a load of bologna at wholesale prices, right from the packing plant in Juarez, and drive it back to Albuquerque. You can be down there and back in one day."

"And how much would this trip pay me?"

"Five hundred bucks. That's nearly a dollar a mile."

Lucky tried to keep any reaction off his face. He could use five hundred bucks. He was stone broke.

"How many rolls of bologna would that be?"

"Thirty," Garcia said.

"*Thirty*? How am I gonna hide thirty rolls of bologna? I couldn't even *fit* that many in my car."

Lucky drove a twenty-year-old Ford Mustang with peeling blue paint. He could barely fit his folded six-foot-three-inch frame behind the wheel. The Mustang had almost no back seat, and a trunk big enough to hold a case of beer.

"We'll supply a vehicle," Garcia said. "A truck."

"And if I get busted? The feds might let me go, but they'll confiscate that truck as well as the load."

"We're willing to take that risk."

"For bologna."

"We've got special clients," Garcia said. "They want Rojo."

Lucky shook his head. Who gets that excited over *bologna*? But he couldn't afford to turn down the job. His current source of income – online fundraisers for phony accident victims – hadn't generated much money lately. People just weren't as charitable as they used to be.

"How soon would I have to go?"

"Tomorrow."

"Jeez," Lucky said. "Not much time to prepare."

"What's to prepare? You drive a truck down to Mexico. You drive it back. We do the rest."

"And you pay me five hundred bucks."

"That's right."

The men stared at each other while Lucky thought it over. Finally, he said, "Let me see this truck."

Chapter 2

Freddie Garcia led the lanky gringo out the back door of the butcher shop, and they both put on dark glasses to defend against the brutal New Mexico sunshine. The shop faced Isleta Boulevard, a few blocks south of Bridge, in a busy area of bodegas and beauty shops and fast-food joints, and the roar of traffic was loud, even behind the brick building. Only a few cars were parked back here – mostly beaters belonging to employees. With its fat tires, the white Chevrolet pickup loomed over the other vehicles.

Freddie watched as Lucky Flanagan walked around the truck, checking its interior and looking underneath at the chassis.

"I don't get it," Flanagan said finally. "You gonna put thirty rolls in the back? Cover them up with something?"

"Open the tailgate," Freddie said. "Look at the bed liner."

The liner that fitted into the back of the truck was heavy black plastic, designed to protect the paint job from the sharp corners of stuff being hauled. Like the rest of the truck, the liner was sparkling clean.

Flanagan bent to examine the black liner where it met the open tailgate. Freddie didn't bother to stoop over. He knew the edge was flawless, the hinges expertly hidden on the inside.

"Looks okay to me," Flanagan said.

"Look closer. The bed liner slopes up toward the cab."

Flanagan crouched to get a better view. The surface of the plastic liner was molded into grooves which narrowed toward the front, assisting the optical illusion.

"I'll be damned," Flanagan said when he finally figured it out. "You've got five or six inches of space under this thing at the front. But the way it slopes back, you can barely tell it."

"It was built special for a drug smuggler," Freddie said. "See that steel ring by the back window? Pull up on that, and the whole liner lifts up on hinges like the bed of a dump truck. We figure there's room for thirty rolls of bologna under there, maybe more."

"Wait a minute," Flanagan said. "What happened to this drug smuggler?"

"He got busted, driving some other rig. This one's never been across the border. Never been on anybody's radar."

"How did you end up with it?"

"The smuggler is married to a woman who's related to my boss. A cousin, I think. She needed to raise money for bail, so my boss bought the truck."

"For hauling bologna."

"I don't know if that was what he was thinking at the time. But you must admit, it's perfect for the job."

Flanagan walked around the truck again, looking it over, shaking his head. The more time he spent with Lucky Flanagan, the more Freddie agreed with his boss' assessment: Lucky was the kind of idiot who always thought he was the smartest guy in the room.

"I don't know, man. Seems like a lot of risk for not much money."

"It's a trial run," Freddie said. "Everything goes smooth, maybe we'll make it a regular deal. You could use five hundred bucks every week or two, right?"

"You can sell that much of this special bologna?"

"We don't actually sell it here," Freddie said. "We deliver it to a few special customers. But other *carnicerías* around the area want Rojo. Like us, they're trying to keep their customers happy."

"So you farm it out?"

Freddie gave Flanagan his hard squint, the one he used to keep employees in line.

"Enough questions. You in or not?"

"Is the truck air-conditioned?"

"Of course."

"What about gas?"

"The tank is full. After that, you're on your own."

"That's gonna cut into my end. A king cab like this gets what, eight miles per gallon? Ten?"

Freddie sighed.

"If you're not interested, I can call somebody else. Plenty of gringos who'd like to pick up five hundred bucks for a day's driving."

"Yes, but none of them as white as me."

"So you'll do it?"

Flanagan nodded. Freddie could see himself reflected in the other man's sunglasses. Two Freddies staring stoically back at him, sweat glistening on their foreheads.

He dug the truck keys out of his pocket and handed them over.

"Take it home with you," he said. "You'll want to get an early start in the morning. I'll call your cell and give you directions into Juarez once you're under way."

"My car will be okay here?"

Flanagan pointed at an aged Mustang. Its blue paint was peeling, and its rear tire needed air.

"I think it'll be safe overnight," Freddie said.

Chapter 3

Lucky Flanagan steered out onto Isleta Boulevard, the truck bouncing on its stiff suspension and oversized tires. He liked sitting up high in traffic, able to see over other vehicles.

The elms and cottonwoods lining the wide street looked wilted in the heat, and Lucky knew just how they felt. But soon, the air blowing from the vents grew cool. Within a couple of minutes, he had to turn down the air conditioner because it was blowing on his left shoulder, making his bursitis ache.

Lucky was only thirty-six years old, but he had bursitis from a car wreck when he was in high school. No big deal at the time, a big purple bruise to show off to the girls. But the doctor had warned that the injury would bother him later, could result in bursitis and arthritis and other ailments that sounded like they only happened to old people. Now, whenever Lucky got a chill, his shoulder reminded him that time was passing.

He had other aches and pains, too, from assorted adolescent injuries. He'd spent much of his teens in splints and plaster casts; his bones just couldn't hold up to his youthful exuberance. He fell out of trees. He fell off roofs. He crashed bicycles and motorcycles and cars, always walking away with nothing more serious than a broken bone or two.

You don't get a nickname like "Lucky" without a lot of scars, the results of near-misses and almost-disasters in your life. If nothing ever happens to you, then you're stuck with your given name, even if it's something horrible like "Edgar," which is what it said on Lucky's birth certificate. But if a lot of bad stuff happens, stuff that easily could have killed you, and you somehow survive, then people will say you must be lucky.

The first person to call him Lucky was his grandfather, who was an eyewitness when lightning struck a cottonwood on the family farm near Bernalillo. Lucky was five years old, a city kid playing in the dirt at the foot of the tree. The lightning strike threw him up into the air and knocked him out cold, but he survived, coming to a few seconds later, no idea what had happened.

"You're lucky to be alive, boy," Grandpa often told him. "You dodged the hand of God."

Two more encounters with lightning when he was in high school made the nickname stick. Once, lightning hit a steel goalpost near him during football practice, stunning half the team. Another time, a thunderbolt struck the car Lucky was driving. Nobody was seriously hurt either time, but he noticed that people started keeping their distance whenever a storm approached. These days, he spent most of the summer thunderstorm season indoors. A man can't be too careful, especially in lightning-prone New Mexico.

As Lucky grew older, the nickname became a burden. People said it with a smirk now that he had proven time and again to be unlucky. He got expelled from school. He got fired from a dozen different jobs. His parents threw him out of their home when he showed no inclination toward leaving on his own. Bad luck seemed to follow him wherever he went, mocking him.

The latest misfortune concerned his marriage. His wife, Jewel, kicked him out of their home six months earlier, and he'd been adrift since, mostly crashing on the sofas of friends. For the past two months, he'd found a home of sorts with an old classmate, Ralph Rolfe, a true weirdo who'd inherited a hundred-year-old house in Albuquerque's Huning Highland neighborhood. The rundown house was cluttered with Ralph's superhero toys and ceramic dragons and other junk, but there was no messy lease.

Jewel had taken up with another man, a rich guy she'd met at work, and she was happy to throw that fact in Lucky's face whenever they crossed paths. Lucky might have accepted a divorce after she acted that way, but there was the matter of their daughter. Scarlett was four years old, smart and chatty and fun. She loved Lucky and needed him in her life. He'd promised he would always be there for her, but it meant taking a lot of sneering abuse from Jewel, who'd decided Lucky was a "loser" who'd never amount to anything.

His track record was on her side. Lucky had fumbled through a series of dead-end jobs and unsuccessful enterprises during their six-year marriage. Jewel earned good money, working in a real estate office, but it was never enough, not when she was paying off his assorted failures.

With little education, a poor job history and no credit, Lucky couldn't rely on the usual sources of startup capital, so he resorted to scams.

For a while, it was the granny scam. He'd find a twenty-something kid on Facebook, a hippie type who "loves to travel," then track down the kid's grandparents through social media connections. Easy enough to turn up Grandma's phone number; old people still kept their landlines listed. Lucky would call her, claiming to be the grandson, and tell her he was stuck in jail in a distant state, in need of bail right away. All a big misunderstanding, and he didn't want to alarm his parents, so if Granny could just wire him the money. . .

A surprising number of old folks fell for the scam, but it still was pretty spotty as a source of income. And it made Lucky feel guilty when he collected the cash.

Then there was the bondage scam. He'd scan the personal ads, looking for local women who said they were into being tied up or handcuffed. Lucky would hook up with a target, go through the motions of a date to get to the point where she was immobilized and gagged, then he'd take his time ridding her home of all its valuables. Unfortunately for him, the word got out in the local bondage-and-discipline community that some jerk was committing such burglaries. He picked up the wrong woman, one who quickly turned the tables on him. Once he was tied up, she beat the ever-lovin' shit out of him, though Lucky shouted the "safe word" the whole time.

The woman had picked the safe word: "Oink." So, when Lucky was in distress, he'd been forced to squeal, "oink, oink, oink," which proved he was a male chauvinist pig or something. He'd lost consciousness before he completely understood the symbolism.

During the resulting hospital stay, Lucky resolved to stick with remote work – using telephones or computers to lift money off victims. People were too dangerous in person.

The latest scam – using internet sites like GoFundMe and Kickstarter to raise money for non-existent medical charities – was becoming increasingly difficult. The fundraising sites had lots of protections against fraud, and it took all of Lucky's ingenuity to circumvent them. As soon as one charity campaign got shut down, he opened another somewhere else. He raked in just enough money to keep him in groceries, never enough to get ahead, certainly never enough to keep Jewel happy.

Now, though he hadn't planned it, he found himself driving up Central Avenue's long, steep incline onto the West Mesa. His old neighborhood was nearby. Jewel still lived in the house they'd shared, and seeing Scarlett meant trudging through Memory Lane in muddy boots.

He told himself he would stop by the house only briefly, just long enough to show off the shiny pickup truck and to tell Jewel that he'd be coming into a little money soon. He didn't expect the gesture to get him anything but the usual lecture about his responsibilities, but Scarlett would get a kick out of a quick visit. She'd always loved "big twucks."

Lucky thought back to what Garcia had said, how using the truck could become a regular event. Five hundred bucks, tax-free, and each trip would only take one day, leaving Lucky free the rest of the time to pursue his entrepreneurial endeavors.

Once he had a regular income, he could rent a place of his own, one where Scarlett could come to visit. Maybe he'd even get back on Jewel's good side.

This could be his ticket into a better life, made possible by people's craving for Mexican bologna. He was happy to give the customers what they wanted, even if it meant crossing the border with contraband. It would be worth the risk to get his life on track.

All he needed was a little luck.

Chapter 4

Jewel Flanagan was cleaning her kitchen, and she heard the truck before she saw it. The picture window in the living room was cracked, and the truck's throaty exhaust made the window tremble and buzz. When the engine noise abruptly stopped, Jewel went to the window to peek outside. She was surprised to see Lucky climbing down from the cab of a shiny white pickup.

Jewel strode quickly through the toy-cluttered living room to the front door of the ranch-style home. She threw open the door and shouted: "If that truck is stolen, I want it off this property right now."

Lucky's face flushed and he glanced around the neighborhood to see if anyone had heard.

"Jeez, Jewel, it's not stolen. Why would you even say such a thing?"

"Then whose is it?"

"Maybe it's mine," Lucky said.

"In your dreams. Where did you get that truck?"

"It's a loaner," he admitted. "I'm doing a job for a guy, and I'm using this truck to do it."

"Yeah?" Jewel narrowed her eyes at him. "What kind of job?"

"Nothing I want to talk about out here in the front yard," Lucky said. "Can I come in?"

"No."

"But I want to see Scarlett. I thought she'd get a kick out of—"

"She's not here. She's spending the evening with my mother."

Lucky made a face. He and Jewel's mother, Rayola, had never gotten along. Rayola had tried to talk Jewel out of marrying him, right up to the day of the wedding, and Lucky had never forgiven her. Rayola's thesis was that Lucky was a lifelong loser and her daughter deserved better, a line of thinking that had begun to appeal to Jewel as the years flitted past.

"Too bad Scarlett's not here," he said. "I know how much she loves trucks."

Jewel tucked her long blond hair behind her ears. She was dressed in denim shorts and a faded red T-shirt with "University of New Mexico Lobos" printed across the front. Her feet were bare, and she pushed aside thoughts of how wrecked her toenail polish looked. Not like Lucky would notice.

"Scarlett's really not into trucks anymore," she said. "It's ponies now. She's got a dozen plastic ponies, and they're all she talks about."

"Ah."

"You'd know that if you spent more time with your daughter."

"I try," he said, "but she's always at your mother's. And I'm not about to go over there—"

"I can't help that," Jewel said. "I've got to work. If I didn't have Mom to help with Scarlett, I couldn't make ends meet."

Why did she bother to lecture him? Words bounced off Lucky like rain off a tin roof. No amount of shame or guilt seemed to faze him. He always had a new idea, another plan, some not-quite-legitimate route to success. He meant well, but he was too self-centered to realize what his scheming did to those around him. And he'd never change.

"I may be able to help a little with money," Lucky said. "Soon. This job with the truck could become a regular thing."

"What kind of thing?"

"Just driving. Hauling stuff. Nothing to it."

Jewel felt sure there was more to that story, but she didn't ask further questions. Sooner she wrapped up this conversation, the sooner Lucky could be on his way.

"I need to finish the housework," she said. "I've got dinner plans."

Lucky frowned. In his trademark black clothes, he looked to Jewel like a sad, skinny mime.

The new man in her life was the exact opposite of Lucky –

well-dressed, successful, sophisticated. He had exquisite taste in food, in wine, in art. And, he liked to say, in women.

Jewel had caught his eye, and she wasn't about to let it go. She had to think about the future. Her future. Scarlett's future. Lucky Flanagan, for all his goofy charms, had no place there.

He seemed to read that on her face. He headed across the sandy yard toward the truck, his shoulders slumped. He stopped after a few steps and turned back to her.

"Tell me the truth, Jewel. Is there any chance at all that we'll get back together? Do you even *think* that way anymore?"

"I think about it sometimes."

"And?"

"Then I come to my senses."

Lucky's face fell, but she was already closing the door.

Chapter 5

The butcher shop had been closed for more than an hour when Freddie Garcia's boss arrived. Only the lights in Freddie's office still glowed inside the shop. He was working late, trying to climb the mountain of paperwork the government requires of an establishment dealing in freshly slaughtered meat.

The boss banged on the back door with the flat of his hand, a rhythmic one-two-three that, Freddie knew, would repeat until someone opened up. He got up from his desk and looked out the window.

Daniel Delgado stood under the lightbulb that dangled above the steel door. He was dressed in a rich brown suit, a slight smile on his face as he banged on the door. His crisp white shirt glowed in the stark light, and his necktie was the deep red of blood.

Freddie and his boss came from the same South Valley background, and were about the same age, but Delgado had silver in his hair and gold in his pockets. He went through the world with an aristocrat's natural grace, as if his feet didn't quite touch the ground. The sight of him in his elegant clothes always made Freddie feel like a peasant, thick of wrist and slow of wit.

Freddie unlocked the door.

"I saw your light was still on," Delgado said. "I need to talk for a minute."

Freddie led the way into the office and moved a stack of papers out of a wooden chair. Delgado folded neatly onto the chair, his legs crossed, and studied his perfect manicure, waiting for Freddie to ask.

"What's up, *jefe*?"

"I was wondering how it went with the new guy, Lucky Flanagan. We on for tomorrow?"

"He went for the five hundred bucks, just as you'd said he would. Seems like a small amount of money for a risky border crossing."

"It's not that risky. That truck is foolproof."

Freddie shrugged. "We'll find out tomorrow."

"What did you think of Flanagan?"

"He seemed kind of stupid, to tell you the truth. Where did you find him?"

"Friend of a friend."

Freddie recognized those as the magic words in Albuquerque, where everything was about friends and family connections. You want to get anything done in this town, you need a lot of friends.

"He's perfect, right?" Delgado said. "Nobody would ever link such an albino to Mexican bologna."

"We'll see," Freddie said. "He didn't impress me as having nerves of steel. He might screw it up."

"He might, but it's a good experiment. We've got to find ways to move more Rojo up the Rio Grande."

"Market keeps growing."

"It's a *craze*. I was at a party the other night, with a bunch of the whitest yuppies you've ever seen, and they were serving fried bits of Rojo on toothpicks. As appetizers. Bologna!"

"*Illegal* bologna."

"That makes it exotic. The host made a big deal of how hard it was to acquire, and everybody got excited to try it."

"Did they like it?"

"They acted like they did. Because it was cool. Everybody was rubbing their bellies and rolling their eyes, so it must be great, right? By next weekend, they'll all have Rojo for their own parties."

"And they'll buy it from us."

Delgado smiled. "Give the people what they want, and they'll keep coming back for more."

"I told Flanagan this might become a weekly gig."

"He like that?"

"You kidding? To a guy like that, five hundred dollars for one day's work is hitting a jackpot. He'll go to Juarez as often as we need him to go."

The boss smiled again, clearly pleased with this minor smuggling operation. It worried Freddie. Delgado seemed a little *too* interested in Lucky Flanagan. How did Flanagan and the boss even know each other? There was a lot that Freddie wasn't being told, and he didn't like that. Too easy to be surprised when you're kept in the dark.

"Flanagan's a temporary solution," Delgado said. "I'm working on a way to get a steady supply of Rojo, enough that we could market it nationwide."

"That big? Really?"

"What if somebody started making Rojo on this side of the border?"

"The recipe is a big secret. That's part of the mystique. And it would still be illegal—"

"Maybe we'd find a way to make it to USDA specifications."

"Wouldn't taste the same," Freddie said.

"That's what they said about New Coke."

"Which was a complete failure."

"It got people talking about Coke again. Everybody had to try it, so they could say how the old formula was better."

"A fad," Freddie said dismissively.

"Fads can pay off big. They don't last long, so you've got to jump on the opportunity right away."

"Then it's over."

"Some percentage of the people who try the product will become regular customers."

Freddie shrugged. The boss knew more about business stuff than he could ever hope to learn. Freddie's world was one of chops and steaks and sausages. In Daniel Delgado's world, those were simply the entrees over which business gets done. Everybody's got to eat, but some people manage to get rich while doing it.

"I hope your new bologna empire doesn't depend on the success rate of Lucky Flanagan."

"You really don't think he can cut it?"

"He might do all right the first run or two," Freddie said,

"but I see a holding cell in his future."

Delgado got to his feet.

"By then," he said, "we won't need him anymore."

Chapter 6

Lucky Flanagan found a parking space around the corner from Ralph Rolfe's place. He made sure to lock up the big truck. He had a spring in his step as he went along the sidewalk to Ralph's house.

This part of Albuquerque, the Huning Highland neighborhood east of downtown, had become gentrified in recent years, mostly populated by hipsters who kept their century-old properties as well-tended as their beards. But there remained a few shabby relics like Ralph's house that had escaped renovation.

The white paint was brittle and chipping away, and the pitched roof had been patched several times with different colored shingles, but at night the house didn't look so bad. Lamps glowed in the living room, throwing a soft yellow light into the screened-in front porch.

Lucky had a key, but Ralph never remembered to lock the doors anyway. The porch was full of dusty old furniture, not much different from the sagging sofas and gut-sprung chairs inside the house. All of Ralph's furniture looked like it once sported a sign saying, "FREE."

The living room was wallpapered in posters of superheroes and space movies, some faded with age. Assorted action figures stood sentinel on shelves and window sills, flexing their muscles. The toys, like everything else in the house, were covered in a fine layer of dust.

Ralph occupied his usual spot on a lumpy brown sofa, facing a flat-screen TV. His blue Captain America T-shirt was pulled tight across his belly, so it was hard to discern that the white blob on the front was a star. Ralph wore the same T-shirt every other day. On the off days, he wore a faded red Flash T-shirt of similar vintage. Other than a wispy fringe of beard that sprouted on his round face in his twenties, Ralph looked the same as he had when they went to Albuquerque High School together, nearly two decades ago.

Ralph had been a clerk at Duke City Comics since high school, and Lucky suspected he still worked for minimum wage. He drove a forty-year-old Plymouth and lived on fast food and ramen and macaroni-and-cheese. If he hadn't inherited this old house, Ralph wouldn't have a roof over his head.

Lucky hadn't been so fortunate in the inheritance department – his parents stubbornly insisted on remaining alive – but Ralph was willing to let him stay rent-free, apparently indefinitely. Lucky thought his pudgy friend had been lonely in this old house. He was doing Ralph a favor, really, staying in his spare room.

The house hadn't enjoyed a thorough cleaning since Ralph's mom passed away years before, and Lucky could feel grit under the soles of his black loafers as he crossed the living room.

"Hey, Ralphie. How's it hanging?"

"Low and slow. You?"

"Doing okay. Got a new gig tomorrow."

He flopped onto the sofa next to Ralph, who hadn't taken his eyes off the TV screen. The audio was off, but the screen flashed with explosions and fire as dwarves and orcs and dragons battled on the screen. Clearly a fantasy game of some sort, but Ralph's hands were empty. How was he playing it?

"What are you watching?"

"*Dragoon of Dragons*. It's a new game, just released."

"You're watching it, but not playing it?"

"It's live, but someone else is playing. A guy in Japan who's already conquered the first twenty levels."

"You're watching someone else play a video game."

"He's doing great so far."

"How long have you been watching?"

"I don't know. Since I got home from work."

"You eat yet?"

"Nah."

"Dude. You should take a break from this."

"I can't right now. He's almost to the Moat of Despair."

"Ah."

Lucky watched the battle on the screen for a minute, then said, "Of all the nerdy things I've ever seen you do, this is the absolute nerdiest."

"I knew you wouldn't get it."

"We should eat something."

"You'll have to prowl the kitchen cabinets. I'm too broke to order out."

"I'm making some money tomorrow," Lucky said. "I'll get groceries."

"That would be great."

"Least I can do."

Ralph still hadn't taken his eyes off the flickering screen.

"Tell me about your new gig."

"Driving a truck down to Juarez and back tomorrow. Five hundred bucks."

That finally got Ralph to look over at him.

"Five hundred bucks? What is this truck hauling?"

"Empty going down there," Lucky said. "Coming back, I'll be carrying some Mexican bologna called Rojo. You ever heard of it?"

Ralph shook his head. His gaze drifted back to the bloody battle on the TV screen.

"Apparently, some people crave the stuff," Lucky said. "They'll pay top dollar for it."

"Huh."

Lucky could sense he was losing his audience.

"It's strictly illegal, of course. Meat processing regulations are much stiffer in the U.S."

He said this like it was common knowledge, but Ralph wasn't buying it.

"Sounds fishy to me."

"Fish is probably the only thing that *isn't* in that bologna," Lucky said. "Don't they make bologna out of the stuff they scrape off the butcher's floor?"

"I think it's made of pig gizzards."

"Chicken lips."

"The anus of the cow."

"You went too far," Lucky said. "Now I'm not hungry anymore."

They watched the battle for a minute, then Ralph said, "Orcs eat every part of the cow, including the horns and hooves. No waste."

Lucky opened his mouth to challenge that statement, but he didn't know where to begin. Orcs weren't real, but cows were. How did they occupy the same world, even in Ralph's boundless imagination? Lucky felt a headache coming on. Talking to Ralph was like hitting yourself in the face with a rolled-up magazine.

"I'm guessing," he said finally, "that orcs like their meat rare."

"Sometimes, they don't even bother to kill 'em first," Ralph said. "They just pounce on 'em and start chewing."

"Lots of realistic snarling and mooing?"

"Oh, yeah."

"You're a sick puppy, Ralph."

Ralph's round face split into a wide grin.

"You have no idea how sick."

"Great. Now I don't have an appetite *and* I'm afraid to go to sleep."

"You have nothing to fear, earthling."

Lucky paused, thinking: *Wouldn't it be great if that were the truth? Had there ever been a time in his life when he had "nothing to fear?"*

He thought about tomorrow: hauling thirty rolls of aromatic bologna past the noses of U.S. Customs and the Border Patrol. Whole lot to fear there. If he started worrying about it now, he'd lie awake all night. That was no good. He needed to get some rest for the long day of driving. He needed to stay calm.

The mayhem on the screen wasn't helping. He forced himself up off the sofa and went toward the kitchen.

Behind him, Ralph said, "Peace be with you, pilgrim."

"And with you," Lucky said automatically.

It was easier to play along with his old friend's quirks than it was to argue. And it was certainly easier than coming up with hundreds of dollars in rent every month.

If this bologna thing became a regular gig, Lucky could get a place of his own. A clean, modern apartment that wouldn't cause Jewel to freak out the way she had the one time she'd seen Ralph's filthy house. If Lucky got a nice apartment in a good neighborhood, Scarlett could spend more time with him and less time under the influence of Rayola, the Wicked Witch of the West.

Handing off Scarlett would mean seeing Jewel more often, too. More opportunities for Lucky to say just the right thing to win her back. If only he could think what that thing might be.

Chapter 7

Inez Montoya liked to start every morning with a soy latte and a cinnamon roll. Neither item was on her weight-loss plan, but she couldn't seem to give them up. This great coffee shop had opened two years earlier, only three blocks from her office, and she'd been a regular ever since. She'd added twenty pounds to her stocky frame in the past two years. Inez was pretty sure the two developments were directly related.

The blue slacks of her uniform were tight at the waist, though she'd let them out only a few weeks earlier. It would be more comfortable to wear the tails of her white shirt outside her pants, the way she did when off-duty, but regulations required her to tuck it in, and Inez followed the rules. She even wore the clunky black leather shoes recommended for her job as a meat inspector, while most of her coworkers wore flashy sneakers.

First time they drop a frozen side of beef on their toes, she thought smugly, *they'll wish they'd followed regulations.*

Inez had learned to keep such thoughts to herself. Early in her career, she'd often blurted out the wrong thing to her coworkers, to the point where they'd begun to think of her as "strange." Nobody likes a bossy-pants, especially one who's completely right about the dress code.

She was nearly forty now, and she'd learned that some things were simply out of her control. The gossip of her coworkers. The temperaments of her bosses. The resentments of the butchers being inspected. All Inez could control was herself. She tried to remember that every day. It had become a mantra of sorts, helping her focus, helping her cope with the unpredictability of other people.

She did her job very well. It was an important job, protecting the public from disease and food poisoning. She undoubtedly saved lives with her diligence. But she often felt unappreciated. Her work was invisible to most people, which meant Inez was mostly invisible, too.

Her uniform and gold badge did catch some people's eye. They took her for a policewoman at first. When they got a better look and saw "U.S. Department of Agriculture," there would be that little smirk. She might as well be a mall cop.

That's why she preferred to enjoy her latte and cinnamon roll alone in her government vehicle, a white Ford compact with a hundred thousand miles on the odometer. She sat behind the wheel, a napkin spread across her shirt. She always parked facing out, so she could watch the parade of motorists who inched past the drive-thru window. Most were undercaffeinated and overworked and on the phone the whole time they waited for their fancy coffees.

Humans in all shapes and sizes, going about their lives, oblivious to her scrutiny. Inez found them endlessly fascinating, but she often felt she was studying a different species, one that didn't include her.

Her work required her to go face-to-face with people all day long. But in those encounters, she was shielded by her badge and her clipboard. She started with the upper hand. She kept a stony demeanor, polite but effective, all business. No time for nonsense.

Now, for instance, she needed to get to her first stop of the day, a thriving butcher shop in the Five Points area of the South Valley. *El Matador Carnicería*. The place had a good record, rarely any violations. But Inez had heard rumors that you could go to *El Matador* for special purchases, such as wild game or whole goats for traditional village cookouts.

Just the sort of thing that can wipe out a whole town at once. Meat that hasn't gone through the proper inspections. Meat that perhaps wasn't butchered and cleaned properly. Meat that wasn't kept at proper temperatures before it reached the public. A zillion microbes and viruses lurk out there, scourges like trichinosis and mad cow disease, just waiting for a chance to attack. Next thing you know, your food is eating you back.

Inez, a dutiful vegetarian, was holding the line against such meat-borne outbreaks. The rest of the population could afford to be frivolous and oblivious, happily tossing back hamburgers and hot dogs, never thinking how their meat could kill them, and it was thanks to serious, focused people like Inez.

She gulped the last of the latte. She touched the napkin to her lips, then stuffed it into the paper cup to soak up any last drops. She worked hard to keep her uniforms clean and crisp; they were as much a symbol of authority as her badge.

When it came to people taking her seriously, Inez needed all the help she could get.

Chapter 8

Lucky Flanagan had been on the road for an hour, squinting against the low morning sun, when his cell rang. The scenery had started to get monotonous – rolling, brushy hills along Interstate 25, the farms of the green river valley to the east, the shadowy mountains beyond them – and the ringing phone sort of snapped him awake. He kept one hand on the wheel while he answered the phone with the other.

"Hello?"

"Good morning, Lucky. Do you know who this is?"

Lucky recognized the deep voice of Freddie Garcia. The butcher sounded just the same on the phone.

"Sure. You checking up on me?"

"Just making sure you got your wake-up call."

"I hit the road an hour ago," Lucky said. "I wasn't sleeping anyway, so I decided to get an early start."

"You nervous? Is that why you didn't sleep?"

"Just kind of excited, you know. First-time jitters."

"That's sounds like nerves to me."

"I'm fine. Making good time."

"Good," Garcia said. "I'll call down south and let them know you're on your way. The plant is on the Chihuahua highway on the south side of the city. I'll text you the street address, but apparently it's a big place. You won't have any trouble finding it."

"And they'll be ready for me."

"They'll be ready. It's a big deal to them. I talked to my boss last night, and he's excited, too. He wants to corner the market on this product, so this could very definitely become a regular job for you."

"That would be great."

"A lot is riding on how you perform today."

"Okay, *now* I'm nervous."

"You'll be fine. If they ask you about the truck at the border, tell them it's a company vehicle. The paperwork is in the glove compartment."

"Okay."

Lucky felt like an idiot. He hadn't even thought to ask about the truck's registration.

"What if they ask me what I was doing in Mexico?"

"*Of course* they'll ask you that." Garcia laughed. "That's what they ask everybody at the border. Haven't you thought up some story to tell?"

"I was busy. But I can come up with something—"

"Tell them you took a load of old furniture to some poor relatives in Juarez. That's why you're driving back empty."

"Hey, that's not bad."

Garcia laughed, but it trailed off in the middle. Sounded like he muttered, "Shit," under his breath.

"You okay?"

"I've got to go," Garcia said. "We've got a federal meat inspector coming in the front door."

The call clicked off, and Lucky put his phone away. He stifled a burp. Nothing but coffee this morning, poured into a stomach that already was full of butterflies. No wonder he had indigestion. Drowned butterflies.

A slow-moving semi was in front of him, so Lucky moved into the left lane. Careful to use his blinker, though he was out in the middle of nowhere. Soon, the big rig was a little rig in the rear-view.

A lifetime of close calls had made Lucky a focused, two-hands-on-the-wheel sort of driver, happy to tootle along near the speed limit rather than pressing his luck in the fast lane. That sounded like the story of his life. Other people passed him by, becoming rich and successful, while Lucky cautiously clanked along in poverty.

It wasn't fair. It wasn't right. But it was the way the world worked.

Only one thing changed a person's lot in life, and that was money. Money can make problems vanish. Money makes everything easier, smoother, less worrisome. Without it, every problem is huge, every snag life-threatening.

Lucky wasted a lot of his time worrying about money. That was no way to live. He needed a steady income, one that didn't require too much work.

Maybe he was onto something now, with the Mexican bologna. Freddie Garcia had talked about weekly runs to Ciudad Juarez, but if Freddie's boss was so excited about bringing in more, they might want to take it up to twice, or even three times, a week.

That would be a lot of driving, a lot of risky crossings, but it would mean a lot of money, too. It might be just the break Lucky needed.

Life in the fast lane, for a change.

Chapter 9

Freddie Garcia had seen the stocky little woman before. A lot of inspectors came through the shop, an assortment of do-gooders and glad-handers, but this woman was the very definition of "no-nonsense."

Freddie felt sure the shop was clean. He had none of the out-of-season elk or wild boar that he sometimes kept on hand for special customers. And no Rojo. Until Lucky Flanagan got back from Ciudad Juarez (assuming he made it back), *El Matador* was out of the Mexican bologna business.

These thoughts sailed through Freddie's head as he hurried to the front of the shop to greet Inez Montoya with a big smile.

Everyone else in the shop kept their heads down, as if the uniform represented Immigration rather than Agriculture. All of Freddie's workers had the proper paperwork and most were American citizens, but old habits die hard.

"Ms. Montoya, I believe," Freddie said, after a confirming glance at the name tag above her shirt pocket. "How are you today?"

"Fine, thank you," she said stiffly, as if someone had taught her that was the proper response.

"Is it time for an inspection already?"

"Not on my schedule," she said. "But I would like to speak to you in private."

"Of course. Follow me."

Freddie led her through the work area to his glassed-in office. As they passed the cutting tables, he said, "Feel free to look around while you're here. We keep everything clean and up to date at all times."

"I should hope so."

Freddie chuckled, but he laughed alone.

"I just meant, we're always ready for a surprise inspection."

"I told you, that's not why I'm here. I'm checking out a rumor I heard from some of your competitors."

Freddie sat in the swivel chair behind his desk, still smiling as the woman sat across from him. He straightened his shirt, which was black with red stitching around the yoke. The shirt always made him feel a little gaudy, as if he should be playing a guitar.

"What sort of rumors are they spreading?"

"That you traffic in specialty products."

"What does that mean? 'Specialty products.'"

"Wild game, which you're not licensed to sell. Products from south of the border that are illegal in the United States."

Freddie gave her the wide eyes. "We have products like that here in the shop?"

"I don't expect—"

He leapt to his feet. "I didn't know about this. Let's go out there and you can show me which products are too special to sell."

"Sit down, Mr. Garcia. You're being ridiculous."

"But if I've got this stuff on the premises—"

"If you did, one or more of your employees likely slipped it out the back door while we were talking in the front. I know how these things work, Mr. Garcia. I've been at this job a long time."

Still standing, Freddie turned to the windows looking out into the employee parking lot.

"I don't see anyone out there with armloads of meat," he said. "You want to go outside and look for them?"

"Sit down, Mr. Garcia."

He sat, swiveling around so he could rest his elbows on his desk.

"You say I'm being ridiculous," he said calmly. "But it's just as ridiculous to come in here chasing rumors. Especially rumors spread by my competitors. This place is successful because I run it correctly, not because I'm breaking any rules."

"Maybe so, but—"

"Not maybe. I'm telling you how it is. Nine-tenths of my job is making sure my people follow the regulations and filling out the endless paperwork required by the government. I suffer from permanent writer's cramp. It was easier when I was cutting meat."

The inspector studied her clipboard for a moment, as if she needed a prompt for what was to come next. When she looked up at him, there was fire in her eyes.

"I'm talking about something serious here. Do you understand what it could mean if one of your little imports was tainted with something? Formaldehyde, say, or lead? Happens all the time in Mexico. People get sick from these uninspected products. People die."

Freddie nodded, but said nothing.

"I'm not accusing you of anything," she said. "I don't even want to look in your freezers. I just wanted to warn you that people are talking about you. About what you're willing to do for your special customers."

"I can't help what people say."

"No, but you can make sure it's not true. Perhaps something is going on behind your back. If one of your people is crossing the line, you must stop it."

"Of course."

"If there's an outbreak of illness, and I trace it back here, I'll close this place down. And I'll do it in such a public way, it'll be a permanent closure."

"You can do that? Permanent?"

"You might reopen," she said, "but it'll be too late. Your reputation will be shot."

Freddie stared at her. He didn't trust himself to say anything.

"Do I make myself clear?" she said finally.

"Crystal clear." His voice sounded ragged in his own ears.

"All right then." She got to her feet. "I guess that's all for today."

Freddie stayed in his chair.

"Thank you for stopping by," he said. "Close the door on your way out. I've got work to do."

Chapter 10

The Rojo plant was a low, windowless building with a dusty asphalt parking lot and a concrete loading dock. Like many other large businesses in Ciudad Juarez, the whole operation was surrounded by a wall topped with jagged shards of broken glass that glinted in the sunshine. The one gap in the wall could be covered by a rusty steel gate that rolled into place, but the gate stood open now, and Lucky drove the smuggling truck right inside.

He understood about security against theft, but this place looked like they were preparing for the Great Sausage Riots. Lights, cameras and barbed wire on the roof. Uniformed security men sweating at the front door.

Lucky drove up to the loading dock unchallenged. As he climbed out of the truck, a rust-streaked door opened and three men came out onto the dock to meet him. One was a guy in his seventies, bald and scrawny, wearing a pale linen suit over a yellow polo shirt. The other two were scowling, muscled-up monsters, who looked to survive on a strict diet of steroids and nails.

One was two inches taller than the other, but otherwise they were identical. They both had shaved heads and they wore jeans and plain white T-shirts with the sleeves ripped away to display the ornate tattoos that decorated their bulging arms. Black tattoos crawled up their necks, too. Mostly, the tattoos were words, but they were in Spanish (which Lucky could barely parse) and written in a Gothic script that would only surrender its meaning under thorough examination. Lucky didn't intend to get that close.

"You must be Lucky," the old man said. He pronounced the word "looky," but Lucky didn't correct him.

"That's me," he said as he went up the steps to the loading dock. "Right on time, despite the traffic jam getting across the bridge."

The old guy glanced at his gold wristwatch, then shrugged, as if time didn't matter much here in Mexico. He reached out his bony, heavily-veined hand for Lucky to shake.

"I am José Villa," he said in lightly accented English. "One of the founders of the Rojo brand."

"A pleasure to meet you," Lucky said.

He glanced over at the two tattooed freaks, but Villa didn't bother to introduce them.

"These two," he said, not trying to hide his disdain, "will load your truck. Let's talk in the shade while you wait."

Lucky followed Villa to a corner of the loading dock which was shaded by the walls. Ten degrees cooler in the shade, though still too hot for his taste. The wedge of shade was barely big enough for them to both enjoy its benefits, and they ended up standing close enough that Lucky could easily hear the old man, though he spoke barely over a whisper.

"Our new hires," Villa said, distaste clear in his tone. "Their job seems to be standing around all the time, looking dangerous. Maybe we'll get some work out of them today."

They watched as the taller of the two skinheads drove an open Jeep up to the rear bumper of the pickup truck. The shiny brown Jeep had a winch mounted on the front bumper, and the smaller skinhead grabbed the end of the cable and unreeled it as he climbed up into the bed of the pickup.

"Those two are the Barreras brothers," Villa said. "Tino and Tito."

"Which one is which?"

"Does it matter?"

Lucky shrugged.

"Everyone calls them the Badass Brothers. They're what you Americans would call 'thugs.'"

"That was the impression I got. All those tattoos."

Villa nodded. "They've spent a lot of time behind bars."

The badass in the back of the truck had lots of slack in his cable now, and he tossed it over a girder that jutted from the wall over their heads. He caught the hook dangling on the end of the cable and attached it to the steel loop on the bed liner. The other brother, meanwhile, had gotten out of the Jeep and moved to the controls of the winch.

Neither had said a word.

"They work well together," Lucky said. "Are they twins?"

"They share the same brain," Villa said. "Unfortunately, neither of them seems to have a conscience."

"Why did you hire them?"

Villa's face tightened for a second, then he said, "It was not my decision. My new partner said we needed more 'security.'"

"You have a new partner?"

"The son of my old partner." Villa sighed. "I started this company forty years ago with my friend Roberto Rivera. We make lots of different products, but the bologna became everybody's favorite. We called it 'Rojo,' from our first names. *Ro*-berto and *Jo*-sé. You see?"

"*Sí.*"

Villa raised an eyebrow and continued in English.

"Roberto died last year and his son, Marco, took over his half of the business. Since then, we've been 'exploring ways to expand our reach.'"

"Including today's little operation?"

Villa shrugged his narrow shoulders again. "Not my idea, but now that I see this truck, I think it'll work."

The winch whined, the cable went taut and the hinged bed liner lifted like the back of a dump truck. The steel bed underneath was perfectly clean.

"Nice," the old man said. "It ought to hold thirty rolls just fine."

He said something in clipped Spanish to the Badass Brothers, who scowled in return. They went inside the same door they'd come out earlier. Lucky imagined it was cool inside the building, refrigerated for all those meat products. But nobody seemed inclined to invite him indoors.

The sky above them was bleached white by the sun, and heat waves shimmered above the parking lot. The minutes ticked past slowly.

Villa leaned forward to look past Lucky at the steel door. "Where did those idiots go? What are they doing?"

As if in answer, the door swung open and the brothers emerged, one of them pushing a wheeled metal cart stacked with rolls of bologna, each a little bigger than a loaf of bread and rounded on the ends. Their red wrappers glistened in the sunshine.

"Are those frozen?"

Villa's eyes widened.

"Rojo is *never* frozen. They're cold, though."

"Will they keep for hours? I mean, it's a four-hour drive back to Albuquerque and it's really hot today—"

"They'll keep each other cold enough. Don't worry about it. Some places down here, they don't even have refrigeration. They just hang the bologna from a rafter on the ceiling."

"It doesn't go bad?"

"Cold is better, but these will be okay. You'll see."

As the brothers started arranging the rolls in the truck bed, the loading dock door opened again and a short, well-built guy came out to greet them. Like Lucky, he was dressed all in black – polo shirt, jeans and cowboy boots – and his swept-back hair was black, too. But, man, was his smile white. It looked expensive.

"Marco Rivera," he said, extending his hand to Lucky, who was nearly a foot taller than him. As they shook hands, Lucky could feel the fat gold ring Marco wore on his pinky.

"Lucky Flanagan."

Lucky didn't like all this sharing of names, but he hoped it meant the beginning of a long-term business relationship.

"I see you're nearly loaded," Marco said. "Nice truck."

"It's not mine," Lucky said. "Belongs to the boss."

"Ah. How is your boss? Doing well?"

"Doing just great," Lucky said, but his mind was whirring, trying to think of some way to trick Marco into saying the boss' name.

"I haven't seen him since our college days," Marco said, not helping at all. "Give him my regards."

Lucky said he would, and they shook hands again before Marco went back inside where it was cool.

The tattooed brothers lowered the bed liner over the rolls of bologna, and the black plastic liner clicked into placc. No gap, no bulge, no way to tell anything was hidden underneath.

One of the brothers climbed up into the bed, stepping gingerly, but the fully braced bed liner didn't sag under his weight. He unhooked the cable from the loop, and the other brother ran the whining winch to retrieve the loose cable.

Time to go.

"Nice visiting with you," Lucky said to Villa.

The old man nodded, saying, "Good luck at the border."

"Thanks."

Lucky went down the steps and around to the driver's side of the truck. He had to walk past the two brothers, who stood beside the Jeep, silently glaring at him. He'd seen such baleful eyes before – on pit bulls.

The brothers made him nervous, which wasn't the best frame of mind for a border crossing. Lucky opened the door and slid behind the wheel. He started the truck and wheeled it around to point toward the gate.

The Badass Brothers didn't move, which meant Lucky had to steer around them. For a second, he considered running them over, making the world a better place. They watched as he pulled away, as if still expecting him to make a wrong move.

He eased the truck through the gate, pausing only a second at the busy street before he gunned the engine and swung out into a gap in the Juarez traffic.

Chapter 11

Traffic crawled over the bridges over the Rio Grande, every lane full of vehicles creeping toward the border inspection stations. People honked and yelled greetings out of their car windows. Street urchins hustled between the stopped vehicles, hawking newspapers and flowers and water bottles to the stalled motorists. Pedestrians chattered among themselves on the wide sidewalks, laughing about how they made better time than the cars.

Lucky Flanagan sat high in the pickup truck, windows rolled up, air-conditioner blowing, nerves humming.

He wore his black wraparound sunglasses, though they were too big for his face and made him look like an anemic insect. The sunglasses were good camouflage for his eyes, which darted all over the place, checking cars, sweeping the pedestrians, searching for trouble. He could feel sweat on his forehead, though it was cool in the truck's cab. He wiped the perspiration away with his thumb.

Nerves. It didn't help that he had to wait so long to go face-to-face with border inspectors. When he'd driven away from the Rojo plant, he'd felt confident. But the longer this took, the more anxious he felt.

What if the inspectors caught onto him? Garcia had said that no one went to jail over Mexican bologna, but Lucky had no way of knowing whether that was true. Maybe they busted bologna smugglers these days, and prosecuted them fully, as a way to stem the fad.

Lucky did not want to spend any more time behind bars. He'd done a couple of stints when he was younger, just a few months, county time, but that had been enough to persuade him that prison life wasn't for him.

Even if he didn't go to actual prison for bologna smuggling, there still would be the initial humiliations of the criminal justice system. The strip search. The cold shower. The fingerprinting and photographing. The coveralls and shower shoes. The jeering of the other inmates.

He kept telling himself everything would be fine. The bed liner hid the bologna rolls perfectly. No reason for a border inspector to get snoopy. But what if they had sniffer dogs? The dogs were trained to hunt for drugs, but might they go ape over the scent of spicy sandwich meat?

By the time he was nearing the inspection station, Lucky was freely perspiring, though he had the A/C turned on high. His muscles were tense, but his brain felt strangely detached. He'd run so many arrest scenarios through his head, the present didn't even seem real anymore.

The inspection stations resembled a row of tollbooths. A metal roof stretched over them, providing a stripe of shade where the inspectors worked amid clouds of exhaust fumes.

Lucky watched as a khaki-uniformed inspector quizzed the driver of the green sedan in front of him. The beefy inspector wore sunglasses and white rubber gloves and a wide-brimmed hat and a frown. Whatever the motorist told him must've been satisfactory because the inspector waved him through. Then he crooked a finger at Lucky, who pulled into the shade and stopped.

As his window hummed down, a blast of hot air rolled into the cab. The wind smelled of car exhaust and diesel and dust. At least he couldn't smell any bologna.

Lucky got out his wallet to show his driver's license to the grim-faced inspector. A label over the officer's shirt pocket said, "SCOTT." Lucky wondered whether that was his first name or last name.

"Good afternoon, Mr. Flanagan," Officer Scott said as he looked at the driver's license. "What have you been doing in Mexico today?"

Lucky fumbled the answer, though he'd been rehearsing for hours.

"Furniture. Old furniture."

Officer Scott cocked an eyebrow above his dark sunglasses.

"I was taking some old furniture down here to some relatives."

"Your relatives?"

"Not mine, my boss' relatives. I don't even know 'em, really. I just drove the load down here so—"

"You didn't buy anything?"

"No, sir."

Officer Scott stood on tiptoe to look over into the empty bed of the truck.

"Where are your ropes?"

"My what?"

"Your ropes. Didn't you have to tie down that furniture?"

"Oh, I see. When they took the rope off the furniture, some kids grabbed it up and ran off with it."

"Hm-mm."

Officer Scott took a flashlight off his belt and shined it into the jump seat in the back of the king cab. Lucky tried to sneak a deep breath, attempting calm, while Scott wasn't looking.

"All right, sir," Scott said abruptly. "You have a good day."

It took a few seconds for Lucky to register what the officer said. He shifted into "drive," then said, "Thank you!"

Lucky escaped into the bowels of downtown El Paso, taking a couple of quick turns so the bridge was no longer in sight. He drove in the general direction of the freeway, taking his time, catching his breath, smiling his ass off.

He'd done it. He'd succeeded. He was now officially a bologna smuggler.

And he'd soon be five hundred bucks richer.

Chapter 12

Freddie Garcia laughed out loud when he saw the big white truck pull into the parking lot at *El Matador*. Despite Freddie's worst apprehensions, the skinny redhead had made it back to Albuquerque. Now, if he had thirty rolls of Rojo bologna with him, the operation would be an unqualified success.

Freddie got up from his desk and went out the back door, propping it open just as Lucky Flanagan unfolded from the cab of the truck. He shook hands with Lucky, who wore black sunglasses to match his stifling black clothes. Lucky looked twitchy, still burning off the effects of the smuggler's high, but he was smiling.

"How did it go?"

"Real smooth. They asked me a few questions at the bridge, but barely looked over the truck. At the inland Border Patrol station, north of Las Cruces? They didn't even stop me. Just waved me through."

Freddie shook his head, which suddenly felt hot inside, pressurized.

"What's the matter?"

"I've gone through those Border Patrol stops a hundred times over the years," Freddie said. "Guess how many times they've 'waved me through?'"

The smug smile slipped off Lucky's face. He shrugged.

"Zero," Freddie said. "They question me every time. Make me show my citizenship papers. Every goddamned time."

"That's too bad, but I don't—"

"You ever hear the term 'white privilege?' This is a perfect example. The boss was right. Send a gringo to the border, and he sails right through."

"You really think that's what it is?"

"What else?" Freddie said. "You got a nicer smile than me? A better job? My family has lived in Albuquerque for three hundred years, but I still get treated like a wetback."

"Do you think it's deliberate? Like, whatchacallit, *profiling*? Or is it subconscious?"

"Which would be worse?"

Lucky pursed his lips as he thought it over.

"People are assholes."

"You'll get no argument from me," Freddie said. "But I'm glad you made it back in one piece. Fully loaded?"

"Yeah. And we probably ought to get it into a cooler as quick as we can."

Freddie went over to the back door and stuck his head inside. All the butchers looked busy, but he called three by name, and they set down their knives and cleavers and headed his way, wiping their hands on their blood-speckled aprons.

Freddie turned back to Lucky and said, "Back the truck up to that roll-up door over there. We'll use that pulley to lift up the bed liner."

Within minutes, they had the truck bed open, and the three brawny butchers were carrying armloads of slick, red-wrapped bologna through the open door to a walk-in cooler inside the butcher shop.

As he and Lucky watched the men work, Freddie said, "Those rolls aren't very cold anymore, but I think they'll be okay. In the future, you might drive a little faster on your way back."

"There's a 'future?'"

"I think we'll want you to take regular trips down south over the next few weeks. You up for that?"

"Same pay?"

Freddie squinted at him. "Is it not enough?"

"No, that's fine. I'm not trying to negotiate with you. Just making sure I understand everything."

Freddie reached into the pocket of his pressed Wranglers and pulled out a roll of fifties.

"Here's five hundred bucks' worth of understanding," he said as he handed the roll to Lucky.

As he slipped the money into his own pocket, Lucky said, "It worked. I can see clearly now."

The butchers lowered the bed liner into place. Job done, they went back inside.

Freddie and Lucky walked over to Lucky's dusty Mustang.

"How soon will you want me to go again? I'm pretty much free for the next week or so—"

"Let me talk to the boss," Freddie said. "I'll call you. Soon."

Chapter 13

Jewel Flanagan was having an unquestionably bad day. Hassles at the real estate office where she worked. A run in her hose. A call from a collection agency. Her ten-year-old car was making a funny noise. And, now, no sooner had she arrived home than her mother was dropping off Scarlett, whose freckled face was crimson from crying.

"What's wrong?" Jewel said as they came in the front door.

Scarlett broke from her grandmother's grasp and ran across the living room in her little pink sneakers. She threw herself at Jewel's legs, hugging her thighs tight and boo-hooing into her crotch.

"You're raising a little brat," Rayola said. "That's what's wrong. She saw the ice cream place as we were turning off Coors Road. I said 'no ice cream before dinner,' and she pitched a fit. You'd think I'd crushed her every dream."

"You don't have to be mean about it," Jewel said. "She's four years old."

"Old enough to know better. She's a brat."

That got Scarlett bawling again.

"Must you say every cruel thing that pops into your head?" Jewel said to her mother.

"Oh, I was just joking."

"Don't you think sarcasm is wasted on a four-year-old?"

Rayola rolled her eyes. She wore thick eyeglasses which made her blue eyes look bigger than actual size. Jewel had suffered that eye roll her whole life. She wished she could keep Scarlett away from her mother's influence, but she couldn't afford all-day child care. She remembered the call earlier in the day from the collection agency. She couldn't afford *anything*.

Jewel peeled Scarlett off her linen skirt, which was now dotted with snot and tears.

Super, she thought, *another dry-cleaning bill*. But she didn't roll her eyes.

Instead, she bent so she was nose to nose with her daughter and said, "Don't listen to her. You're not a brat. You're a sweetheart. Grandma's just tired."

Rayola scoffed, but Jewel didn't look up at her.

"Thanks for bringing her home, Mom."

Her mother harrumphed, but she turned toward the door.

"See you tomorrow," Jewel said to her back.

Just as Rayola reached the door, the bell rang.

"You expecting somebody?"

"No."

Rayola threw open the front door, standing squarely in the doorway, a fireplug in a calico dress. Past her head, Jewel could see Lucky on the porch. His hands were full – a bottle of wine and a bouquet of supermarket flowers – and he had a big smile on his face until he registered Rayola standing there, blocking his way.

"I was just leaving," she said.

"Good."

He stepped aside to let her pass.

They're like two cats, Jewel thought, *circling and spitting*. Hate at first sight, and it's never going to get any better.

"Daddy!"

Scarlett ran to Lucky and gave him the same sort of crushing super-hug she'd given Jewel. From the way Lucky's eyes widened, Jewel suspected Scarlett had crashed into his crotch a little too hard. But he couldn't react, not with his hands full. Jewel relieved him of the flowers.

"For me?"

"Wine, too, if you feel like opening it."

She took the chilled bottle from him and carried it into the kitchen. Scarlett chirped at him in the living room while Jewel put the flowers in a glass vase. She opened the white wine, then carried two full glasses into the living room. She handed one to him and joined him on the sofa. They clinked glasses.

"What are we celebrating?"

"I had a successful day," Lucky said, "and I thought I'd

spread the wealth a little."

They sipped their wine, but she kept watching him, waiting for him to reveal more. Scarlett sat on the carpet at his feet, looking at him with adoration in her eyes. It made Jewel's heart hurt; the girl loved her daddy.

"This was that driving job you mentioned?" Jewel asked. "In that big white truck?"

Lucky nodded. "I got paid in cash. Five hundred bucks."

"Not bad."

"Looks like it'll become a regular gig, too. I could be driving down to Juarez once or twice a week."

"You went to Juarez."

"That's right. Didn't I mention that before?"

"To do what?"

"Just driving, like I said."

"You took that truck down there."

"Right."

"And you drove the same truck back?"

"Yep."

"And the truck was empty both ways?"

"Well . . . "

Jewel told Scarlett to go to her room. When the girl whined, Jewel said, "Get your new pony so you can show Daddy."

Scarlett clambered to her feet and trotted off down the hall. As soon as she was out of earshot, Jewel turned on Lucky.

"What did you bring across the border in that truck?"

"You wouldn't believe me if I told you."

"Was it illegal?"

"Technically, but you can't get sent to prison or anything."

"Oh, really."

She stared at him until he cracked.

"Okay, I'll tell you about it, but it's a secret, all right?"

They both looked down the hall, but Scarlett was still out of sight.

"It's bologna," Lucky said.

"I beg your pardon?"

"Mexican bologna, this brand called Rojo. You can't legally get it in the States, so people are willing to pay ten times the normal price for it."

"You're shitting me."

"That's what I said! But apparently it's a hot market."

Jewel thought about that for a moment, then the obvious answer hit her.

"Nobody is going to pay you five hundred dollars to smuggle *bologna*. That's nonsense. There must've been something more profitable hidden in that bologna."

Lucky blinked at her a couple of times.

"Did you see the bologna with your own eyes?"

"Sure. I picked it up at the factory."

"In Juarez."

"Right."

"Did it seem odd in any way?"

"The bologna looked fine, all sealed up properly. A couple of tattooed thugs loaded it up, but otherwise it was just a simple business transaction."

"What if there was something hidden in that bologna?" she said. "Drugs or something."

"No, I'm sure that—"

"Maybe they played you for a fool," she said. "Maybe you smuggled cocaine or heroin into the country and you didn't even know it."

Lucky shook his head. "It's not like that. It's just bologna."

"How can you be sure?"

Chapter 14

Inez Montoya hung up her uniform as soon as she got home. The blouse was a little wrinkled, but Inez thought she could get another wearing out of it. Once her uniform and clunky shoes were put away, she slipped into her usual at-home outfit – shorts and sandals and an oversized T-shirt, this one a garage-sale find advertising a brand of tequila she'd never tasted.

Inez went into the kitchen, trailed by her two cats, Boo and Hiss. So far, she'd acted like she hadn't noticed them meowing in her wake. Both cats were strays that had adopted her – Boo a sleek black male and Hiss a scrappy tabby female – and they weren't the most affectionate pets. But she always had their full attention at mealtime.

Once the cats were munching away at their bowls, Inez got a Miller Lite from the fridge and went into the living room of her ground-floor apartment. She flopped onto her sofa and put her feet up on the coffee table.

"Long day," she said aloud, and one of the cats meowed from the kitchen, as if in answer. That made Inez smile.

She'd visited seven businesses today, conducting inspections and measuring meat temperatures and making notes on her clipboard. On her feet, or in and out of the car, all day long. Plus, there was her first stop at *El Matador Carnicería*. She didn't plan to write up a report on that encounter. She'd warned Freddie Garcia, and that was enough. For now.

Inez sighed and sipped her beer, slowly relaxing. Every workday, she felt she carried the safety of the public on her shoulders. Only when she was home could she let that burden go.

She flipped on the television, and surfed through channels, the sound off. Nothing much there to snag her gaze, but the cats joined her in the living room, licking their chops and staring at the flickering images on the TV screen.

Inez finally settled on a soccer game. She didn't know who was playing, but she found it soothing to watch grown men in shorts running up and down a green field. So soothing, in fact, that she dozed off after five minutes of silent soccer.

When she jerked awake a few minutes later, a sportscaster was interviewing one of the players, a skinny man who puffed for breath as he answered the post-game questions. The player was darkly handsome, but you could tell he knew it. His hair was cut to fall perfectly across his forehead, even when sweaty, and his mustache was a thin line along his upper lip.

Freddie Garcia had a thin mustache like that. Inez wondered how they managed it. Some kind of clippers? A razor? She ran her fingers over her upper lip, where there was a little peach fuzz, nearly invisible. Inez kept an eye on that nascent mustache. Her mother had a similar one, and hers turned thick and dark as she got older. By the time she went off to the nursing home, she looked like Groucho Marx. Inez would take up shaving before she let that happen to her.

She'd never kissed a man who had such a manicured mustache, and she wondered how it would feel against her lips. A stiff bristle? She wouldn't like that. Be like kissing a toothbrush. Maybe, it was such a thin line, you wouldn't feel much at all. Maybe, if you were caught up in the kissing, you wouldn't even notice.

Long time since Inez kissed anybody. Nearly seven months. And that kiss had come at a New Year's Eve party, so it shouldn't even count. Give some people enough champagne and they'll kiss anybody at midnight.

Inez finished her beer. She needed to get up and make a veggie burger, but she felt so pooped, she couldn't manage it right now. She set the empty bottle on the end table and slumped lower into the sofa.

Soon, with the cats watching over her, she dozed off again, twitching with dreams of Freddie Garcia's mustache.

Chapter 15

"Then what happened?" Ralph Rolfe asked.

"Jewel asked how I could be sure there wasn't cocaine or something in that bologna," Lucky said.

"Good point. What did you say to that?"

Lucky shrugged. He seemed to be doing that a lot lately, as if he kept encountering things he couldn't understand. Ralph knew just how that felt.

"I finished my wine," Lucky said, "and I admired Scarlett's new pony toy. Jewel kept looking at her wristwatch. It felt awkward, you know? Like it was time for her to start putting dinner together, but I wasn't invited."

"Time for you to go."

"Exactly. I left the flowers and the rest of the wine and I said good-bye and I came back here."

"Was Scarlett upset that you left so soon?"

"Not much. I think she was hungry."

Ralph said in a girlish voice: "Hey, Mom, make this guy get out of here so we can eat."

"Something like that."

Lucky turned up the beer bottle, chugging until it was empty. Ralph took a sip in camaraderie, but he didn't really like plain beer. He liked fruity drinks, something with lots of Vitamin C, but he'd never say that to Lucky. Beer was manlier. At least Lucky seemed to think so.

Ralph often used Lucky to judge such things. Ralph was a lifelong nerd, destined to always be out of step with society, and he was okay with that fate. But Lucky was a man of the world. Ralph felt fortunate to have such a friend.

"Jewel kind of took the fun out of the whole thing, huh?"

"She's great at that," Lucky said. "Couldn't let me enjoy my newfound gig even a little bit before she started casting shadows over it."

Ralph nodded, trying to look understanding. He wasn't

always able to convey his emotions through his face, and people often got the wrong impression. He'd learned to wear a vague smile most of the time. It fit his round face. Lucky said it made him look like he was quietly passing gas, but better for people to assume you're happy or glad to see them or even blissfully farting than to think you're some kind of dangerous weirdo.

Lucky seemed lost in thought, so Ralph waited. He wore his Flash shirt today, and he picked at the yellow lightning bolt on his chest. The decal was peeling around the edges. The red T-shirt had faded to pencil-eraser pink over the years, but Ralph couldn't bring himself to replace it. It was his favorite.

"You know the one person who bugs me in this whole thing?" Lucky said abruptly.

"Jewel?"

"No."

"Rayola?"

"Well, yes, but that's not—"

"Scarlett?"

"No, man, she's—"

"I know," Ralph said excitedly. "The butcher guy! Garcia."

"No, would you just let me—"

"The old guy at Rojo!"

Lucky had gone red in the face. "Stop guessing!"

"Oh, okay. Sorry."

"You'd never guess it anyway. Because we don't know who he is."

Ralph had no idea what he meant.

"The big boss," Lucky said. "I don't know who he is, and Garcia has been real cagey about him when I've asked."

"And that worries you?"

"Garcia said his boss saw me somewhere and thought I'd be perfect for the smuggling gig."

"Because you're so very Caucasian."

"Right. But where did he see me? How does he know me?"

"Does it make a difference?"

"Maybe not. The money spends fine, no matter what. But

can I trust these people when I don't know who the boss is?"

"What if the boss *is* a drug dealer?" Ralph said helpfully. "Then you really would need to worry about something being hidden in the bologna. Just like Jewel said."

Lucky frowned, but he didn't get a chance to reply, as Ralph was hit by an inspiration.

"You know what Batman would do?"

Lucky's blue eyes went wide for a second, then he sighed in surrender.

"What would Batman do, Ralph?"

"He'd watch the butcher shop to see who comes and goes. If the big boss owns the place, he must stop by sometimes."

Lucky surprised Ralph by saying, "That's not bad."

"Really?"

"Garcia's office has windows, so I could see whoever meets with him, if I get in the right position. He's seen my car, but if I park down the street, he might not notice."

Nothing vague about Ralph's smile now. He was thrilled that Lucky considered his idea. He was about to suggest a black cape for night-time surveillance, but Lucky changed the subject.

"I have cash for once," he said. "Shall we order a pizza?"

Ralph clapped his hands together twice.

"We shall, good sir, we shall."

Chapter 16

Wednesday morning, Lucky tried to focus on his fundraising scams, but he was distracted, thinking about bologna smuggling.

He set up on the sofa as soon as Ralph went off to work at the comic book store. Laptop in his lap. Coffee within reach on the end table. Phone in hand. He was dressed in gym shorts and a black T-shirt and flip-flops. Perfect conditions for working at home, where every day is Casual Friday.

His latest fundraising campaign was nearly ready to go – a poor eight-year-old girl named Jessica needed money for life-saving kidney surgery – but Lucky couldn't settle on a photo to lead it off. Millions of photos of eight-year-old girls on the Internet. Thousands of girls who looked frail enough to portray the mythical Jessica. Lucky scrolled and scrolled, to the point where his unfocused eyes no longer registered the parade of photos on the screen.

He couldn't keep his mind off Mexican bologna. Driving to the border and back was a lot easier than coming up with a Jessica story and all the accompanying crap – starting the donation site, setting up the bank account, circumventing the protections used by the websites to prevent scams just like his. And all of it would vanish as soon as Kickstarter or GoFundMe caught on to him. Sometimes, the same day as when he'd done the work. It could be frustrating as hell.

Bologna smuggling, on the other hand, required only a few minutes of stress, while actually crossing the border. The rest was cruising along I-25, enjoying the New Mexico scenery. About as easy as a job can get.

He knew he was glossing over the nervous parts now. When he was facing that grim border guard, he'd nearly burst with anxiety. But it was only a few minutes of torture. And it had to get easier with practice, right?

Lucky pictured two trips a week, hauling bologna to Albuquerque. That would be a thousand bucks in his pocket.

With that much coming in every week, he could soon afford to buy a smuggling truck of his own.

Because Lucky didn't plan to work for Freddie Garcia and his mysterious boss for long. As soon as he had his own rig, he'd negotiate a price with José Villa and start his own smuggling enterprise. He could make a lot more if he didn't have to split the profits with the *El Matador* bunch.

He'd have to make contacts among the butchers, find out who would pay top dollar for Rojo, but he could distribute it himself. Might have to rent cooler space somewhere, but he'd still come out way ahead.

At heart, Lucky was an entrepreneur. He wanted to build a business of his own, but one that wouldn't eat up his life. This bologna enterprise fit the bill. He could make a tidy sum before the fad fades, then get out of the smuggling business with enough of a grubstake to start something more legitimate. A pawn shop, maybe, or one of those payday check-cashing places. A man could make a good living off other people's misery, but he needed money to get started.

Once the business was up and running, all he'd need was an employee or two to operate the cash register. He could sit at home and count his money.

That was the lifestyle Lucky had always pictured for himself, leisurely managing a business empire. Could it all be within reach now, thanks to Mexican bologna?

Chapter 17

Freddie Garcia had been at work for an hour when his boss showed up at the butcher shop.

Daniel Delgado looked as sleek as usual, wearing a dark gray suit with a white shirt and a black bolo tie. He worked the room as he made his way through the shop, shaking hands and speaking to each of the employees.

He always looks like he's running for office, Freddie thought. *Taking a moment to look people in the eye, earning their loyalty for the price of a smile.*

After five minutes or so, Delgado reached the door to Freddie's office. He knocked, though he clearly could see Freddie through the glass, waiting for him at his cluttered desk.

"Come in!"

"Hi, Freddie. Got a minute?"

As if Freddie had any choice.

"Sure, boss. Sit down."

"I can only stay for a minute," Delgado said as he perched on the edge of the wooden chair. "I've got other stops to make."

"I'm glad you came by. I've got some papers for you to sign."

"Good. I'll take them with me."

Freddie set the slim folder on the corner of his desk nearest the door, so they wouldn't forget.

"We had a federal meat inspector come by here yesterday," he said. "A woman named Inez Montoya?"

Delgado shook his head to show he didn't know her.

"Anyway, she gave me a stern warning about dealing in wild game or selling anything from south of the border."

"Really?"

"Somebody told her we were doing that, but the shop was clean when she was here, so she's got no proof."

"Did she search the place?"

"No. Just wanted to warn me. I acted like I didn't know what she was talking about, of course."

"Of course." Delgado smiled. "She didn't mention Rojo specifically?"

"No. But we should've been more discreet when we were wholesaling it."

"Don't worry about it," Delgado said. "Without proof, she's got nothing."

"She's watching us. Trying to catch us in the act of moving Rojo through here. I think we ought to cool it for a while."

That smile again.

"I was thinking just the opposite. I've got a butcher in Colorado Springs who's dying to get his hands on some Rojo. Let's make another run to the border right away."

"You sure?"

"I've got friends at the Department of Agriculture's office here. If this inspector becomes too much of a nuisance, I'll get her fired."

Freddie nodded, but he thought it likely wouldn't be that simple.

"You want to use the gringo again?"

"Lucky did a good job, right? He's eager for more?"

"Do we want to send that same face across the border again so soon? We use him time after time, and somebody eventually will recognize him and figure it out."

Delgado stood and smoothed the front of his suit, ready to go.

"Thousands of people cross that bridge every day. The odds are on our side."

No sense pushing our luck, Freddie thought, but he said, "I'll arrange it right away."

Delgado picked up the folder of papers from the corner of the desk and turned toward the door.

"Thanks, Freddie. I knew I could count on you."

Always so damned polite. When you're rich, you can afford to be gracious.

Freddie watched through his windows as the boss charmed

his way out of the shop, every head turning to return his smile. The folder was under his arm as he went out into the bright sunshine.

Freddie sighed. He already had too much to do today, and Daniel Delgado had just dropped another chore on him. So smoothly, he'd hardly felt it.

Chapter 18

The real estate office where Jewel Flanagan worked was in a boxy brick building on Lomas Boulevard near San Mateo, one of the busiest intersections in Albuquerque. Hardware stores, drug stores, thrift stores, supermarkets, fast-food joints and a full-service car wash all competed for motorists' attention with a colorful forest of franchise signs and flapping flags. Jewel's quiet office was tucked among all that noise, and Lucky drove past it every time.

Catching himself, Lucky braked and pulled into the parking lot of the next business, a taco joint where nobody would notice an extra car in the lot. He left the Mustang in an out-of-the-way slot and picked his way through the spiny landscaping that separated the two asphalt lots.

Hot already, so he was glad to step through the tinted doors of the real estate office. It was blessedly cool inside, and he paused a moment to savor it, his eyes closed behind his black sunglasses.

"Lucky? What are you doing here?"

Not only did Jewel do tons of paperwork for the firm, but she also served as de facto receptionist since her desk was the one customers encountered first. *Ought to be good for business*, Lucky thought. She looked great, in a plum-colored dress and twinkly earrings, her blond hair pinned back on the sides. The sight of her was a punch in the gut.

"Hi, there," he said, taking off the sunglasses. "I was in the area—"

That was a total lie. He'd been sunk into Ralph's couch until thirty minutes ago.

"—and I thought I'd stop by and see if I could take you to lunch."

The smile slipped off her face.

"That's sweet, Lucky, but I already have lunch plans. Sorry."

He tried to keep the disappointment off his face.

"I should've called first. But, like I said, I was in the neighborhood—"

"Doing what?"

"What?"

"What were you doing?"

"What do you mean?"

"You were in this part of town. Why?"

"Oh, um, I, uh, needed to stop by the hardware store, and pick up something for Ralph."

"More problems at that wreck of a house?"

"You guessed it."

"That place is going to fall down around your ears."

"I don't plan to be there much longer," Lucky said. "Now that I've come into some regular money, I'm going to get a place of my own."

"Really? That would be nice."

"Then Scarlett could visit me more often."

Jewel smiled. "We'll see."

He knew that meant "no," but he didn't want to pursue it now. He turned toward the door, saying, "Maybe another time on lunch."

"Maybe so."

He went back out into the glaring heat, fumbling to put on his sunglasses. He stalked across the asphalt and gravel to where he'd left his Mustang baking in the sun.

Lucky got behind the wheel and cranked up the engine and turned on the air conditioning. He latched his seat belt to make the chiming stop, but he didn't put the car into gear. He just sat there, watching Jewel's office, waiting for her lunch date to arrive.

He remembered what Ralph had said about Batman, doing surveillance like a detective. Was that what Lucky was doing now? Or was he simply spying on his estranged wife? That surely would be the way Jewel saw it, if she caught him out here.

A low, sleek car purred into the lot of the real estate office. European sedan, silver with black windows. Lucky didn't know much about luxury cars; they were too far out of his price range to even dream about.

The car parked near the front door, and the driver's door opened. A fit-looking, forty-something man climbed out of the car. He wore a gray suit and a white shirt that stood in bright contrast to his coppery skin. His black hair glinted with a sprinkle of silver.

The man went inside Jewel's office. Lucky waited for him to come out, though he dreaded what he expected to see.

The elegant man emerged moments later, holding the door open for Jewel. She was laughing about something as she stepped outside, her teeth bright in the sunshine, and it made Lucky's heart sink.

So this was the rich boyfriend. How in the hell was Lucky supposed to compete with a guy like that?

The man opened the car door for Jewel. Lucky ducked low in case she looked his way, but she only had eyes for her new beau.

A stabbing pain in his jaw told Lucky he was grinding his teeth. He opened his mouth and rocked his jaw back and forth, trying to work the cramp loose. Then he started his car and followed them. They only went about a mile, trailing Lucky. He knew he shouldn't get too close, but at a red light he was right behind them. That close, he could read the logo that said the car was a Jaguar. *Damn.*

Lucky had never heard of the bistro where they went. He parked up the street in the lot of a boarded-up bookstore and waited for Jewel and her date to reappear.

More than an hour passed before they emerged from the café.

"Pretty damned leisurely lunch," Lucky muttered to himself as they walked to the Jaguar. They were holding hands, and that made him grind his teeth some more.

He figured they were going back to Jewel's office, so he let them get a big lead, then cruised over there. He arrived just as the man was giving Jewel a kiss on the sidewalk out front. It was a pretty chaste kiss, just a peck really, but it nearly caused Lucky to lose his mind.

He circled the block, coming back to the real estate office in time to follow the Jaguar away.

Lucky guessed that the boyfriend would go back to his own job, and he hoped that would help him learn the guy's name. He followed him onto the freeway and was surprised when the Jaguar headed to the South Valley. The river valley has its share of rich folks living among the farming families who've been there forever, but Lucky guessed there weren't many Jaguar drivers. Who *was* this guy?

He nearly lost him in traffic on Bridge Boulevard, but he caught up as the car turned onto a side road lined by homes. Just as Lucky was turning, too, the Jaguar veered into a long driveway that led to a sprawling adobe home, just the kind of place Lucky would expect a Jaguar driver to live.

Lucky went past the driveway, driving until the house was out of sight, then turned around to go back the way he'd come.

He slowed as he passed the guy's house, and a truck behind him honked in impatience. Lucky sped away, but he'd seen what he'd hoped to see: A name on the mailbox next to the street.

The mysterious boyfriend had certainly made the name easy for the postman to spot. Bold black letters on a white background: DELGADO.

Chapter 19

Inez Montoya pulled up in front of the *Carne Grande* butcher shop a little after 4 p.m. Her last stop of the day. After this, she'd go back to the office and finish up the paperwork on today's inspections. With luck, she'd be done by dinnertime.

Carne Grande was north of downtown, in a Mountain Road neighborhood that has gentrified in recent years. Several restaurants sit among the old pitch-roofed houses, and condos are springing up along Twelfth Street. The butcher shop was decorated in the red and green of Old Mexico, but Inez thought most of the customers were white yuppies looking for "authentic" experiences. Just the sort of place that might slip some illegally processed meat into the inventory as an exotic lure.

Inez got out of her car, straightened her uniform, checked her clipboard, and marched through the front door.

The shop was owned by two clean-cut brothers named Hernandez – Rick and Raul. They were Mexicans who'd immigrated to the United States as teens. They worked hard and they kept their shop clean. Inez didn't expect to find any problems.

Rick was alone behind the counter, wiping the top with a white cloth. As she approached, he casually tossed the rag into a large cardboard box sitting open near the cash register.

"*Buenos tardes*," he said, smiling. "Is it really time for an inspection again already?"

She held up her clipboard in answer.

He laughed. "Seems like you were just here."

"It's a regular rotation. Your turn came up."

"Do what you need to do, Inspector. I'll just put this stuff away."

He lifted the cardboard box and started to turn away, but Inez said, "Hold on. Let me see that."

"This?"

"Just set it down."

His face flushed, but he did as he was told. Inez lifted the rag and looked underneath. The bottom of the box held three bright red rolls of bologna bearing the "Rojo" label.

"What do we have here?"

"Nothing," he said, still looking embarrassed. "I mean, nothing to do with the shop. Little something for personal use."

"You're not selling it?"

"No, I swear. I know it's illegal."

"Then where did you get it?"

"I bought it off someone. Just for us. Raul and I grew up eating this stuff. Fry it up, wrap it in a warm tortilla. It's a delicacy."

"So good that you need three big rolls of it?"

He shrugged. "Sometimes, we share with our friends. But I promise you, we've never sold it out of the shop."

"It was sitting next to the cash register."

"Only because I was putting it away. I swear—"

"Where did you get it?"

Hernandez clamped his mouth shut, and his expression went stony.

"Tell me," she said, "or I'll have to assume the worst. I'll have to assume that you brought it into the country illegally, and that you were planning to sell it."

"That's not true."

"Doesn't matter what's true, if you don't cooperate. Tell me what I need to know, and it can go easier for you."

"Easier like we forget the whole thing?"

Inez shook her head.

"Easier like maybe we pay a fine, but you don't shut us down?"

She nodded.

Hernandez stared off into the distance, deciding. Behind him, a few employees peeked through the narrow windows of the swinging doors that led into the work area of the butcher shop. They whispered among themselves, but no one came out to see what was happening.

Finally, Rick Hernandez shook his head.

"I can't do it. The guy I got this from, he's a big shot. I turn him in, and he'll run me out of business."

"What do you think I'm going to do?"

He frowned. "You might try, but you've got rules to follow. We can appeal, whatever. It'll cost me in legal fees, but we'll still be in business."

"We'll see about that." Inez tucked her clipboard under her arm and picked up the box. "Don't move. I'm going to put this in my car as evidence. Then I'm coming back in here, and you and I are going over this whole place with a fine-toothed comb."

Hernandez sighed.

"If I find so much as a trace of Rojo anywhere else in this building, you're history."

"You won't."

"We'll see."

Chapter 20

Freddie Garcia liked the feel of the smuggling truck. It handled well for such a large rig, and it stood tall in traffic. He felt like he was riding a big white stallion.

The sunset sky was a watercolor painting of pale yellows and pinks. Hardly any clouds, no relief from the heat. Freddie found himself praying for the thundering rains of the summer monsoons that usually started this time of year. Not a sign of them so far.

The office workers had already fled downtown for the day, and it was too early for the crowds that swarm the Central Avenue bars at night. Freddie steered through the empty canyons between downtown skyscrapers and made his way across the railroad tracks to the old Huning Highland neighborhood.

Didn't take long for him to find the address Lucky had given him over the phone. He could've probably picked it out on his own; it was the shabbiest house on the block. Exactly the kind of place he'd expect to find Lucky Flanagan.

Lucky must've been waiting on the porch because he came out the screen door before Freddie even pulled to a stop. He hurried to the truck like he didn't want Freddie to come inside the house.

"Let's do it," Lucky said as he climbed into the cab.

"Aren't you going to invite me in?"

"What?"

"Ask me inside, offer me a beer?"

Lucky squinted at him. "I thought you were in a hurry."

"I am," Freddie said. "I'm just messing with you."

He put the truck into gear and eased away from the curb. No traffic in this quiet neighborhood.

"Mess with me all you want," Lucky said. "Won't hurt my feelings. I'm in too good of a mood."

"Looking forward to another trip to Juarez?"

"It's not a bad drive," Lucky said, "and I like the money."

"Sure you do."

They rode in silence for a minute, then Lucky said, "So what did he say? Your boss with no name. He must've been happy with my performance if he's ready to go again so soon."

Freddie managed to keep from smiling. Lucky amused him, fishing for compliments like a girl.

"He said you did just great," Freddie said. "And he specifically asked that you be the driver again."

"Really?"

"You already know where the Rojo plant is, and how it works. Use a different bridge over the Rio Grande when you come back this time, but otherwise everything is the same."

"Sounds good."

Freddie went faster this time, using Interstate 25 to go south. He got off at Cesar Chavez Boulevard to drive down into the valley to where he'd left his car at *El Matador.*

Freddie still got a weird feeling about the boss and his interest in the smuggling operation. Not that much profit in it, so why does Daniel Delgado even care about expanding the bologna market? And why does he insist on Lucky's involvement?

He glanced over at the redhaired man. Lucky had a smile on his face, still pleased with his performance evaluation.

Idiot.

Chapter 21

On Thursday's drive down to Ciudad Juarez, Lucky found himself looking forward to chatting again with Rojo founder José Villa. But this time the cranky old man was nowhere to be seen.

The Badass Brothers were there, though, waiting on the concrete loading dock. He parked the Chevrolet pickup beside the dock, same as before. The tattooed brothers started rigging up their Jeep winch before he could even get out of the cab. The heat was brutal, and Lucky felt slapped in the face by it as he emerged from the truck.

The Badass Brothers didn't give him so much as a nod as he went up the steps of the loading dock. He went over to the same sliver of shade he'd previously shared with José Villa, and stood waiting for the loading to be over.

The back door into the building opened a minute later. Marco Rivera strode out onto the loading dock, clamping black sunglasses onto his face.

He was dressed in black again, same as Lucky, but Marco also wore a lot of gold – necklaces and rings and a fat gold watch that glinted in the sunshine. But what captured Lucky's attention was the shiny pistol stuffed into the front of his waistband. Lucky got a tingly feeling on the back of his neck, like all the hairs there were standing up and looking for an exit.

"Ah, it *is* you!" Marco said as he came over to shake the taller man's hand. Lucky tried not to loom over him. "I couldn't believe it when they said the redhead was back so soon. You must really love your Rojo!"

The speech felt *performed,* as if Marco thought they were being taped or filmed. Lucky looked around quickly. He saw no sign of surveillance equipment, but you wouldn't, would you? It would be tiny, hidden from sight, recording their every word.

"I sure do," he said lamely.

Marco laughed and slapped him on the shoulder, which made Lucky flinch.

"Move over a little, my friend."

Lucky shuffled to the side so Marco could share the shade. They stood shoulder to shoulder, watching the Badass Brothers do the work.

"Where did you get those guys?" Lucky asked

"Prison," Marco said.

"Excuse me?"

"They got paroled at the same time last year, so I hired them both."

"Ah."

"We try to do our part to help such men get rehabilitated," Marco said. "It's our civic duty to employ them."

Lucky glanced over at him, saw that Marco was smiling at his own bullshit. At least he recognized it for what it was.

"What's with the gun, Marco?"

"This?"

Marco yanked the pistol from his belt and waved it around, making Lucky want to dive for cover. But there was no place to hide. Nothing but concrete and asphalt, hard surfaces good for producing ricochets.

"Hey—"

"We have to stay ready at all times," Marco said, shutting one eye to aim down the barrel at the white truck. "We have many enemies."

"In the bologna business?"

Marco cocked an eyebrow at him. "On the streets. Juarez is a dangerous town."

"You afraid the poor will riot?"

"No, never." Marco looked puzzled, as if that thought had never occurred to him. He stuck the gun back in his belt. "But there are thieves everywhere."

"Thieves who'd steal bologna?"

"People want our secret recipe. It's the most valuable thing we own. Nobody else can make Rojo."

The Badass Brothers came back outside with the rolling cart, one holding the door open for the other. They rolled the cart over to the edge of the dock and started loading the glistening red rolls into the bed of the pickup.

"Your boss," Marco said slyly, "is he trying to make his own Rojo?"

"What?"

"Maybe he orders so much because he's trying to figure out the secret recipe."

"He's just reselling it, as far as I know. Turning a profit."

"Not too much of a profit. Not on thirty rolls."

"It's a specialized market," Lucky agreed. "But there's a growing demand."

"Of course," Marco said. "Once you've had Rojo, no other bologna will do."

"That sounds like your new advertising slogan."

Marco laughed. "It could be!"

The tattooed brothers were finished loading the bologna now, and the winch whined as it lowered the bed liner back into place.

"Such a fancy truck for such small-time smuggling," Marco said.

Lucky started to tell him what Freddie had said about how the boss had come to acquire the truck, but Marco was already onto something else.

"You'll drive straight through, back to Albuquerque?"

"That's the plan. Why?"

"It's a hot day," Marco said. "We don't want that Rojo to spoil."

"I'll drive fast," Lucky said.

Marco laughed and slapped him on the shoulder again. Lucky wished he would stop doing that. The surprise contact made him jump every time.

"You seem nervous, Lucky. Are you okay?"

"I'm fine. Just ready to hit the road, that's all."

"Go right ahead," Marco said. "And give my regards to your employer."

Lucky muttered that he would, but he was thinking how he

still hadn't managed to identify the man at the top. He went down the steps and climbed into the sun-heated cab of the truck. He cranked up the throaty engine and turned the air conditioner on full-blast.

A last glance over at the loading dock, where Marco Rivera and the Badass Brothers stood squinting into the sun, watching him go, then Lucky got the hell out of there.

Chapter 22

Lucky took his time driving the unfamiliar streets of Ciudad Juarez, deciphering the signs as he made his way to the Zaragosa bridge ten miles downriver. The border crossing there was a much smaller operation, aimed at trucks carrying agricultural products and cheap factory goods. He told himself he should be able to sail right through, but something Marco Rivera said still bugged him.

The Chevrolet king cab *was* an awfully nice truck to risk for bologna. With its specialized bed liner, it could be really useful to people smuggling across something more valuable. Drugs, say, or gems or guns. If Lucky got caught with a load of Rojo, the government would seize the fancy truck forever. For a few thousand dollars' worth of beef and pork byproducts in bright red wrappers.

It just didn't make sense.

Was something hidden inside that bologna, as Jewel had suggested? Was he being set up?

Lucky spotted a hardware store that looked just like the Home Depots back home, a giant warehouse surrounded by an asphalt lot full of pickup trucks. He jerked the wheel, turning across two lanes to whip into the parking lot. Horns blared behind him, but he ignored them. He was a man on a mission.

Inside, the store seemed familiar, even if the signs were in Spanish, and he cast about for what he needed. Aha! There, not far from the entrance, he spotted a display of braided nylon clothesline. Not too thick, but probably strong enough to do the job.

He carried a cellophane-wrapped coil up to the cash register and paid for it with two crumpled dollar bills. The plump cashier smiled slyly, as if she knew he was up to something with that rope.

Lucky hurried out of the store, back into the blazing sunshine, and crossed to the Chevy pickup. He drove out of the parking lot onto a side street, which quickly emptied into a dusty neighborhood of old adobe houses that appeared to be melting into the ground from whence they came.

He went several blocks into the neighborhood before he found what he needed: A sturdy old cottonwood with a thick branch that reached out over the street. He pulled over to the side of the narrow street and sat there for a minute, thinking how to do the job.

No other traffic along this dusty street the whole time he sat there. Five grimy children lined up on the shoulder across the street from him, picking their noses and staring at the big white truck, but none dared come closer.

Lucky used his pocketknife to slice open the package of clothesline, then got out of the cab. The truck was partly in the tree's shade, but it didn't seem to help. The temperature was close to a hundred degrees. And he was the idiot wearing black clothes.

As the children watched, he climbed up into the back of the pickup and tied the white cord to the steel loop behind the cab. Couple of extra knots as insurance, then he turned and tossed the coil over the overhanging branch. Got it on the first try, the spool of clothesline landing in the street behind the truck.

Lucky looked around as he climbed down from the bed. Only the children seemed curious about him. Uncoiling the line, he walked backward until he reached a utility pole ten feet away. He wrapped the line around the wooden pole a few times and tied it off.

He got behind the wheel and cranked up the engine. A gust of air-conditioning hit him in the face, and it felt like a blessing.

Lucky put the truck into gear and let it creep forward, ever so slowly. The nylon clothesline went taut as he inched forward, and the bed liner began to lift. Once the black plastic blotted out the view through the back window, he stopped the truck and put it in park.

As he climbed out of the pickup, he realized the children were clapping their filthy little hands, tickled by his trick with the skinny rope.

The bed liner was raised just far enough that he could snake an arm in there and fish out a roll of Rojo. He hesitated. The clothesline was taut as a guitar string. If it snapped, so would his arm.

Lucky glanced over his shoulder. The children had stopped cheering and were watching intently, waiting to see what he'd do next. He didn't want to let them down.

He took a deep breath, inhaling courage, and reached under the bed liner. The Rojo was cold and slick, but he managed to tip up one roll so he could grab it with both hands and yank it through the gap.

More cheers from the peanut gallery.

Lucky got back into the truck and set the Rojo on the passenger seat. He put the truck into reverse and backed up slowly, letting the plastic bed liner set gently down onto his hidden cargo. He watched in the mirror as the clothesline went limp.

He hated to get out of the air-conditioned cab again, but he couldn't go anywhere tied to a telephone pole. He climbed up into the bed and sliced the line off the steel loop.

Once he was back in front of the air-conditioning vents, he took a moment to catch his breath. Then he used the pocket knife to slice through the red wrapper of the bologna roll. He sawed away at the bologna, opening the roll stem to stern. Nothing inside that looked like drugs. Nothing, in fact, but Mexican bologna.

Lucky sliced off a sliver of the multicolored meat and popped it into his mouth. Pretty damned tasty. Saltier and smokier than American bologna, sort of like summer sausage. He'd had nothing to eat for hours, so he ate a few more chunks of Rojo. Then he used the knife to slash repeatedly across the whole roll, making sure nothing was hiding inside.

Nada.

Lucky mooshed the roll back together as best he could, then rolled down his window. The kids across the street had been watching the whole time, licking their chops. Lucky whistled, and the largest of the kids – a skinny boy about ten – cautiously approached the truck.

Lucky reached the bologna down to the kid and told him to take it to his *mamacita*. The boy nodded and hurried away, pursued by two of the others. Lucky put the truck into gear, watching in the rear-view as two other boys scuffled over the clothesline he'd left behind.

Burping, and feeling comfortable that his cargo included nothing but Rojo, Lucky headed for the Zaragosa bridge. The line of traffic was much shorter than the lines downtown, and Lucky rolled up to a border officer within minutes.

The officer was a hefty African-American woman who filled out her khaki uniform to the bursting point. Her hair was slicked into a bun, and she wore elaborate eye makeup and purplish lipstick. Her name badge, which sat high on her prominent bosom, said, "JOHNSON."

"How are you today, sir?"

"Just fine, thanks." Lucky handed over his license and registration. "And you?"

"Another exciting day on the border," she said flatly as she scanned his documents. "This is a company vehicle?"

"Yes, ma'am. I drove a load of furniture down from Albuquerque for my boss. Delivered it to some of his poor relations in Juarez."

The story had worked beautifully on the other officer, but he must've sounded too rehearsed this time because Officer Johnson cocked an eyebrow at him.

"You have a bill of sale for this furniture?"

"No, ma'am. It was a gift. You know, charity."

"Hm-mm. You came through here with a load of furniture? I didn't notice any furniture going over the bridge."

"I went over the downtown bridge."

"But you're coming back this way. Why is that?"

"Turned out the relatives lived closer to this bridge. I thought it would be the faster way home."

She shook her head. "Long way out of your way, if you're going to Albuquerque."

"Like I said, they live right over there, not too far from this crossing."

"Uh-huh." She handed back his documents. "Why don't you pull over to that parking slot right over there?"

She pointed to one of several slots angling away from the main flow of traffic.

"Is something wrong?"

"I want to look over your truck."

"Okay, but it's empty. I didn't buy anything in Mexico."

"You didn't go shopping while you were over there?"

"No," he said, stifling another burp. "I just had lunch."

She recoiled, making a face, and Lucky realized she must've gotten a whiff of his bologna breath. He coughed into his fist, but it was too late.

"Pull over to that parking slot, sir. And turn off your engine."

Gulping, Lucky did as he was told. His window was still rolled down, and the wind streaming inside was hot and dry. He hated to give up the air-conditioning, but he killed the engine and watched in his mirrors as Officer Johnson got another officer to take over her post. Then she walked toward Lucky, snapping her white latex gloves so they fit tighter on her hands. Lucky's sphincter clenched in dread.

"Pop the hood, please," she said as she passed his window.

He pulled the lever, and the hood bumped open. Officer Johnson found the latch and opened the hood the rest of the way, blocking Lucky's view to the front. He waited anxiously while she checked every cranny around the engine.

Then she worked her way around the rest of the truck, running her gloved hands over every surface and checking underneath with a mirror on a long steel rod. Lucky nearly pissed himself when she got interested in the edge of the bed, but the tilted plastic liner stood up to inspection, and she eventually moved on to the wheel wells.

Finally, after ten minutes or so, Officer Johnson returned to his window. She was puffing from exertion and seemed disappointed.

"All right," she said. "You're free to go."

She turned and walked away, her big hips swaying, leaving Lucky to shakily get out of the truck and close the hood she'd left open. Then he got back inside the cab and eased into traffic, eager to get away from the border.

Chapter 23

Inez Montoya knew she was in trouble as soon as she got the message from her boss. She'd just sat down to type up her daily reports, trying to wrap up the workday, when up popped an e-mail that said, "See me."

She cleared the screen, then walked to the corner office of Lou Duran. She could feel her coworkers watching her, but she didn't give them the satisfaction of any kind of emotional reaction. Cretins.

Inez tapped on the glass set into Lou's office door, and he called out from inside, "Come in!"

As usual, Lou's desk was buried under stacks of reports and requisitions. He'd told her once that he expected to get caught up on his accumulated paperwork approximately five years after his death. Which, from the looks of his flushed face, could be any minute now.

"What's the matter, Lou?"

He took a deep breath through his nose, calming down, and tilted his bald head toward a wooden chair across from him. Inez sat.

"I just got off the phone with Rick Hernandez," he said. "Over at *Carne Grande*."

"I know who you mean."

"He said you kept him at his shop until eight o'clock last night. Is that correct?"

"It was a little after eight, but yes, that's right. I caught him in a clear violation, and I thought that justified a full inspection."

"This violation? That was the Rojo?"

"Yes, sir. He had three rolls there in the shop."

"He says they weren't selling it. It was for their own use."

"That's what he told me, too. But he had it right there in the shop—"

"He said a guy came in off the street and sold it to him."

"That's not what he told me," she said. "He said he got it

from someone who was big enough to put him out of business."

"What do you mean 'big enough?'"

"Ask him."

"I'm asking you."

"Well-connected. He seemed frightened of this person."

"Rick Hernandez? Frightened?"

"Well, worried at least."

"Hmm. That wasn't the impression I got. The only person he seemed upset with was you."

"Excuse me, sir, but I caught him red-handed."

"With a little Rojo." Lou shrugged. "Hardly a headline-making case."

"I'm not trying to make headlines. I'm trying to keep people from eating meat produced under unsanitary conditions."

Lou nodded, but he looked weary.

"I know, Inez. You're very by-the-book."

"Yes, sir."

"But until eight o'clock at night? I didn't authorize any overtime."

"I haven't filed for any. I thought it was important to strike immediately, in case he had more bologna stashed somewhere in the building."

"And did you find any more?"

"No, sir."

"Any other violations?"

"No, sir."

"So you made Rick Hernandez miss dinner with his in-laws because of three rolls of Rojo?"

"Three rolls or three hundred, it's a violation to possess it in this country."

"I know, Inez. I know."

Lou stared at the ceiling for a minute. Inez thought he looked old. The skin under his jaw sagged, and his ears seemed ever larger alongside his bald head.

"Have you ever tasted Mexican bologna?"

"No, sir. I'm a vegetarian."

"I know that, Inez. We all know. I just thought you might've tasted it at some point."

Inez felt herself bristle, but she kept the emotion off her face. She told herself to think about Boo and Hiss. The cats relied on her for survival. She couldn't cast aside her well-paying job.

"If I were tempted to eat meat, it certainly wouldn't be processed bologna from Mexico."

He smiled.

"You don't know what you're missing. It's really tasty when it's fried."

"So I'm told. By Rick Hernandez."

The smile slid off Lou's face and he sighed.

"I told him on the phone that we wouldn't pursue the matter any further."

"I've already written him up, sir."

"For the Rojo, but nothing else?"

She nodded.

"All right. But otherwise let's lay off him, okay?"

"I planned to do a follow-up inspection."

"Of course. But let's give it some time, all right? Let him cool off."

"His emotional well-being is not my concern, sir. I'm only concerned about the welfare of the public—"

Lou stopped her by holding up a hand.

"Just do as I ask, okay?"

"Very well. When should I feel free to return to that shop?"

"I'll let you know."

Inez took a deep breath, settling herself. Not biting her tongue, exactly, but ready to beat a strategic retreat.

"Yes, sir. Whatever you say."

He squinted at her, as if trying to judge whether she was crossing a line with her attitude. She didn't give him the chance to decide.

"Anything else?" she said.

"No, that's plenty for today."

Without another word, Inez got to her feet and walked stiffly back to her desk. She sat facing her computer and battered away at the keyboard, trying to ignore the whispers of her coworkers.

Chapter 24

By the time Lucky Flanagan reached the Border Patrol checkpoint north of Las Cruces, he'd convinced himself that Officer Johnson had snapped to something after waving him across the border and had called ahead to have him detained.

He had no reason to believe this flight of nerves, but that didn't stop him from worrying as he approached the huge metal shed that served as the I-25 checkpoint. A couple of green Border Patrol cars were parked nearby, but all the action centered on four shaded bays where uniformed officers checked vehicles for illegal immigrants and forbidden fruit.

Lucky burped again and tasted acid. That Rojo wasn't sitting well on his stomach. He wondered if you were supposed to cook the bologna before eating it. Maybe that's why those Mexican kids had been so wide-eyed, watching him wolf down chunks of raw bologna. He told himself people ate raw meat all the time without serious consequences. He could survive a few bites of Rojo. Still, he'd stop somewhere soon for antacids.

The truck inched forward, Lucky aiming for the bay with the fattest of the four officers in view. He was a red-faced man whose khaki-covered belly hid his belt buckle. Lucky figured that a fat man would exert the least effort on a hot day. It seemed like a good guess, too, as the sweaty officer motioned the next two cars through with the smallest hand gesture he could manage.

As Lucky approached, though, the officer suddenly got inspired. He held up a hand. Lucky's pulse pounded as he pulled to a stop so his window was squarely in front of the uniformed officer, whose nametag said "JONES."

He hummed the window down and said, "Yes, sir?"

"You bringing any produce into the country?"

"Produce?"

"Fruits. Vegetables."

"Oh. No, sir. I'm not hauling anything.

Officer Jones looked into the bed of the truck, but it was mostly in the sun, and he clearly wasn't leaving the shade. He appeared to be sniffing the air. Good grief, Lucky thought, can he smell that hidden bologna? Is it *cooking* in this heat?

"You just have lunch?"

"Yes, sir. Big, spicy meal at a restaurant in El Paso. Guess I need a breath mint."

Officer Jones nodded. Lucky clamped his mouth shut and tried to breathe through his nose. Jones stood on tiptoe to look over into the bed. Then he stepped back and said, "Okay. Go ahead."

The truck was already in gear. Lucky goosed the accelerator and surged away from the checkpoint a little faster than he'd intended.

He zoomed onto the freeway, then checked his mirrors, half-expecting one of those squad cars to roar to life and chase after him. But they just sat there, getting smaller in his rear-view mirror, until he finally topped a hill and the checkpoint disappeared from sight.

Lucky gasped for air. He hadn't realized he'd been holding his breath.

Chapter 25

Jewel Flanagan was finishing up for the day, stowing her stuff, tidying her desk, when her cell phone rang. She checked the readout. Lucky calling. Should she even answer? The work day had ended okay, and she had big plans for dinner. Why let Lucky ruin the transition?

But Jewel couldn't help herself. She punched the button to answer.

"Hello?"

"Hey, Jewel. What are you doing?"

"I was just leaving the office. What do you want?"

"That doesn't sound very friendly."

"I don't have time to play around, Lucky. I need to get home for Scarlett."

"I was just checking in, you know. Letting you know that I made it across the border again safely."

"You made another run?"

"I'm on my way back to Albuquerque now. Everything's fine."

"I can't believe you, Lucky. Why take such a risk?"

"Five hundred dollars. That's why."

"Couldn't you just get a *job*? There are safer ways to earn five hundred bucks."

"Too many strings attached to jobs," he said. "I'm an entrepreneur. I need to be free to pursue different opportunities."

"Like Mexican bologna?"

"For example. If I'd had a regular job, I wouldn't have been available for this deal."

"If you get thrown in jail, you won't have—"

"I told you, hon. They don't jail people over Mexican bologna. This is practically risk-free."

"Uh-huh."

"You should've seen me today, going through those border checkpoints. Nerves of steel."

"Uh-huh."

"And there's nothing but bologna in this load. I checked one of the rolls, opened it up with a knife. Nothing but meat."

"That's one roll out of how many?"

"Thirty, but I picked it at random—"

"If they're having you smuggle drugs or something, they'd only need to put it in one roll. Put a mark on it so people on the other end would know which one—"

"I'm telling you, Jewel. It's not like that. It's purely a bologna proposition. I pick it up straight from the factory."

"And the people at the factory seem okay?"

A long pause.

"That's what I thought," she said. "You're in over your head again, Lucky."

"I'm just driving. The rest is somebody else's problem."

"So far."

"Boy, you're determined to ruin my good mood, aren't you?"

"Sorry, Lucky. You shouldn't call up like this, expecting me to be happy about what you're doing."

"I was going to offer to take you out to dinner. You and Scarlett. I'll be back in time to—"

"I've got other plans."

"Oh." Lot of disappointment communicated in that one syllable.

She said nothing.

"Wait," he said. "Scarlett was with your mom all day, and now you're dumping her somewhere else?"

Jewel's face felt instantly hot.

"I'm not *dumping* her anywhere. She's going to visit Gail down the street. Gail's got two older girls, and Scarlett adores spending time with them."

"Shouldn't she be spending that time with one of us?"

"Gail's a single mom. She knows what it's like, trying to have a life beyond motherhood."

"You're not a single mom."

"Not yet. If you'd agree to a divorce—"

"I guess I should let you go."

Jewel felt bad, deflating him in his moment of masculine glory. She never should've answered the phone.

"I do need to get going."

"You have a good evening," he said stiffly.

Click.

Chapter 26

By the time the white pickup bounced into the parking lot, low sunbeams angled through the windows of the butcher shop. Freddie Garcia got up from his desk and stretched the kinks out of his back. Sometimes, he thought being a butcher had been easier on his body than all the deskwork he did now.

Freddie's Western-style shirt had pulled loose, and he tucked it tight into his jeans as he went out the back door to meet Lucky Flanagan beside the truck.

"You're late," Freddie said. "I expected you an hour ago."

Lucky was wearing his black sunglasses, so Freddie couldn't read his eyes, but he was quick with an answer.

"Took longer to get across that other bridge. Customs pulled me over and searched the whole truck."

"And?"

"I'm here, ain't I? I thought they were going to search it again at the Las Cruces checkpoint, but the guy finally waved me through."

"Hot day," Freddie said. "I hope your cargo is okay."

"Me, too."

Freddie went inside and got two of the butchers who'd done the job last time. The others had already gone home for the day, and these two were headed that way, too, already in their street clothes. But they followed him out to the back lot, where Lucky had parked the truck under the pulley.

They hauled the bed liner up and started removing the rolls of Rojo. Freddie pitched in this time, so it would go faster. Lucky, standing in the shade in his black clothes, didn't offer to help, which didn't surprise Freddie. Lucky wasn't the type to volunteer.

Freddie and the two butchers carried the Rojo inside to the cooler, three rolls at the time, so Freddie knew something was wrong when he got to the last two rolls in the truck.

"You're short," he said to Lucky.

"What's that?" Lucky came out of the shade to look inside the open bed.

"There's only twenty-nine rolls here."

"Aw, hell," Lucky said. "They must've miscounted at the Rojo plant. I should've counted behind them. Never crossed my mind that they might short us."

"Probably just a mistake. But count the rolls next time."

"Hey, take the missing roll out of my end, if you want. I'd completely understand."

"That's all right," Freddie said. "Just, you know, next time."

"Right."

One of the butchers had come back outside to check on the delay, and Freddie told him in Spanish to take in the last two rolls and call it a night. The weary-looking butcher nodded and did as he was told.

Freddie pulled a roll of fifties out of the pocket of his jeans and handed it over to Lucky.

"There you go. I'll be in touch about the next run."

Lucky nodded and pocketed the money.

Freddie turned to go back inside where it was cool. Behind him, Lucky said, "Um, one thing?"

"Yeah?"

"I don't have my car here. You picked me up, remember?"

"So?"

"So, can you give me a ride home?"

"I just gave you five hundred dollars," Freddie said. "You can afford a taxi."

"Oh, okay. I just thought—"

"I've got work to do."

Freddie went inside, leaving Lucky out in the hot sun. He made sure the back door shut behind him.

Chapter 27

Lucky hadn't used Uber since the last time his Mustang was in the shop, but the phone app still worked, and he summoned a ride. The *El Matador* sign, which stood on a steel pole, threw a square of shade onto the parking lot, and Lucky waited in the protective shadow, sweating. He couldn't see inside the butcher shop because of the sun's glare on the windows, but he got the feeling that Freddie Garcia was watching him the whole time.

Finally, a black Toyota Prius rolled silently into the parking lot and stopped in front of him. The window hummed down and the driver – a forty-year-old Hispanic woman with a purple scarf tied round her head like a pirate – said, "Are you Lucky?"

He had five or six smart-ass answers for that question, but he was too tired to trot them out at the moment.

"That's me."

She peered at him over the top of her huge sunglasses.

"You look okay," she said. "Hop in."

Lucky thought he looked better than "okay," but he knew what she meant. She was answering a call in the South Valley, headed downtown. A driver would have good reason to be cautious.

He opened the back door and slid into the air-conditioned interior, surprised by how much leg room was available behind her bucket seat, which was pulled all the way forward. Lucky realized she couldn't be more than five feet tall, up close to the wheel like that, but she was broad-shouldered and seemed sort of *formidable*.

The inside of the car was spotlessly clean, but it was decorated with dozens of dangling crystals and bundles of sage and holy cards with pictures of sad-eyed saints. It looked like a good place to get your palm read.

He told her the address of his destination, though he'd punched it into his phone already.

"I know," she said. "Get you there in a jiffy."

She zoomed out into traffic, making Lucky fumble for his seat belt. Be a hell of a thing to get killed in a car wreck now, when he had a pocket full of cash.

The driver watched him in the rear-view. He wished she'd watch the road instead, but the electric car seemed to find its own way through the traffic.

"So, your name is really Lucky?"

"Not my legal name. But that's what everybody calls me."

"Why?"

"Why what?"

"Why are you called Lucky?"

"There's a red light coming up."

"I see it," she said, not slowing. "There must be a reason for this nickname."

"I got struck by lightning and lived to tell about it."

"Really?"

She looked a little wide-eyed in the mirror, and Lucky felt strongly that she was too distracted to be at the wheel.

She hit the brakes about then, but the red light changed to green, and Lucky was thrown back into the seat as the car sped forward again. They bumped over a set of railroad tracks, and Lucky was sure they went airborne for a second. He held on tight.

"Three times," he said.

"What?"

"I've had close calls with lightning three separate times."

"Good God!"

"If there were a cloud in the sky right now, anywhere in sight, I'd put you out of the car."

"Well, that seems extreme—"

"I don't want to be near you when it happens again."

"It's not gonna happen again," Lucky said. "I stay indoors during thunderstorms."

"I'll bet you do! If I were you, I might never go outside."

"Accidents happen indoors, too."

"To you?"

"Plenty of times. So far, I've been fortunate."

"Ah," she said. "'So far.' That's the trick, right? You never know when 'so far' is over."

"I usually find out the hard way."

A green light up ahead changed to yellow, and she gunned it to zoom across the wide intersection. Lucky closed his eyes and braced for impact, but they sailed through unharmed.

"You been driving for Uber long?"

"Two years," she said. "I've got a perfect record."

"Maybe *your* name should be Lucky."

"Hah!" She wheeled the Prius around a corner, the car leaning precipitously. Lucky leaned the other way, like he was on a sailboat, as if his one-hundred-sixty pounds would make much of a difference.

"My name is Esperanza," she said as the car straightened out. "It means 'hope.'"

"That's harder to live up to than 'Lucky.'"

"Think so?"

"Luck is sort out of my control, right? But *hope*, man, hope is an act of will. You have to *believe* in something to have hope."

"Don't you believe in anything?"

"I believe in the randomness of the universe. Shit happens, and usually not for any discernible reason."

She took a moment to digest that, then said, "So you have to *hope* the shit doesn't happen to you."

"I guess that's right."

"Which brings us back to luck."

"Or hopelessness. Depends on how you look at it."

The Prius zipped across busy Lead Avenue, cars honking behind them. Esperanza slowed as they reached Lucky's block.

"It's that seedy-looking one on the right," he said.

"Ah."

She pulled to a stop in front of Ralph Rolfe's house.

"Here we are," she said, turning to look back at Lucky. "Safe and sound."

"We certainly made good time."

"That's the secret to success in this business," she said. "Go fast. He who hesitates laughs last."

"I don't think that's the way that goes."

He settled up with her, giving her a nice tip, and climbed out of the Prius. He barely got the door shut before Esperanza zoomed away. Made him feel like counting his fingers to make sure they were all still there.

Lucky stood watching her go until the black car disappeared around a corner. Then he headed up the steps.

A truck rumbled on a nearby street and it sounded enough like thunder that Lucky instinctively hurried to get indoors, though there wasn't a cloud in the evening sky.

Chapter 28

They were halfway through the salad course before Daniel Delgado asked Jewel what was wrong.

"What do you mean?"

"You've hardly said anything since we got here," he said. "And you're picking at your salad like you've never seen one before."

He smiled broadly, flashing his even white teeth. His smile looked expensive, like everything else about him. His charcoal-gray suit, his jewelry, his manicure, his perfect skin. Whenever they were out on a date, Jewel always felt like the second-prettiest one at the table.

She'd worn her nicest black dress tonight, dressing it up with some bangles and beads, trying to look her best for dinner at High Noon, the classic steakhouse in Old Town. The restaurant was in a hundred-year-old adobe building, but the menu was modern and the wine list was superb. Or, at least that's what Daniel said. The pinot noir he'd ordered certainly was excellent.

And now she was ruining the evening, moping.

"Sorry. I talked to my ex on the phone before I left the office. He always sets me off."

"What did he do now?"

She shook her head. "Doesn't matter. Let's not let him consume more of our evening. I'll perk up."

"It's okay," Daniel said. "I'm sort of fascinated by Lucky Flanagan."

Jewel didn't know how to take that, so she said nothing. No need. Daniel was always happy to fill any conversational lulls.

"Over the years," he said, "I've met a few other guys who were called 'Lucky.' They were uniformly the *un*luckiest bastards you're ever going to meet."

"That sounds like my Lucky, too."

"Yours?"

"You know what I mean. It's like he's got a black cloud over his head, following him wherever he goes."

"Don't you think he brings it on himself? I mean, his own behavior gets him into trouble—"

"He was hit by lightning three times," she said. "I don't think you can blame him for that."

Daniel laughed heartily. Even his laugh was perfect. Jewel sometimes thought she could listen to it the rest of her life. Other times, though, she sensed something rehearsed in that laugh, like the schoolyard bully who jokes his way out of trouble when he gets caught.

"Guess that does make him lucky," he said. "If he can survive lightning bolts, he doesn't need a rabbit's foot."

He chuckled some more. Jewel smiled, but she couldn't seem to work up a laugh. Not when it came to Lucky. She wished they weren't talking about him. It touched an impulse to defend her husband, though he was estranged and strange and unlucky as hell. She stifled the urge. Better to let the conversation naturally shift elsewhere.

"I threw some work his way," Daniel said. "Did he mention that?"

"What?"

He glanced around to make sure the waiters weren't listening.

"Has Lucky told you about his recent trips to the border?"

Jewel realized her mouth was hanging open, and she clamped it shut.

"That was you? *You* sent him to Mexico?"

He shifted in his chair, the smile frozen on his face, and Jewel recognized that she'd gotten a little loud.

"Sorry," she said, leaning toward him to whisper. "You *hired* Lucky?"

"Not exactly. An associate of mine was looking for someone to bring bologna across the border. We were talking about how the driver should be a white guy, and I told him about Lucky. Let's face it: Lucky is the whitest guy ever."

"He has to stay out of the sun. He burns easily."

"I'll bet. Anyway, my associate called Lucky and asked him if he'd be interested in making some easy money. From the look on your face, I'm guessing you know the rest."

"It's dangerous," she said. "And you said yourself, he's not a lucky guy."

Daniel scoffed.

"It's bologna. Nobody cares if you bring it into the country."

"Then why is it illegal?"

"*Technically* illegal. If they catch you, it's a fine."

"I don't want him behind bars," she said, and she was surprised at the force in her own words.

Daniel looked surprised, too, his dark eyebrows high on his smooth forehead.

"You still have feelings for him."

"No, that's not it," she said. "He's Scarlett's dad. She'd be crushed if he ended up in jail."

"I thought you'd be happy that Lucky was making some money for change."

"Not if it's risky money. He needs a regular job. Why couldn't you help him get one of those?"

"Lucky doesn't seem to be good employee material. What's his job history like?"

Jewel looked away.

"That's what I thought," he said.

Their waiter glided up to the table, bearing their steaming steaks on platters. He set the entrees before them and vanished again while Jewel was still trying to decide whether her appetite had vanished, too.

Daniel had no such hesitation. He sawed a chunk off his bloody sirloin and popped it into his mouth. He moaned with pleasure as he chewed.

"Perfect," he said. "Try it. You'll see."

She picked up her knife and fork, but didn't use them.

"Tell me the truth, Daniel. Are you setting Lucky up in some way?"

"Of course not. Why would I do such a thing?"

"To get him out of the way. He keeps stalling on the divorce papers—"

Daniel laughed and touched his napkin to his lips.

"Believe me, Jewel, if I wanted Lucky out of the picture, I could take care of it with a phone call."

Jewel felt a chill. "What do you mean?"

"Say I called Lucky and offered him ten thousand dollars to leave Albuquerque and never come back, do you think he'd take it?"

Jewel set down her silverware.

"Probably," she said. "He'd find that much money irresistible."

"And would he keep his word, or would he come back to Albuquerque as soon as he started to miss you and Scarlett?"

She hated to judge Lucky, but she felt sure that's exactly how it would go.

"That's what I thought," he said, reading her face. "If he can't be bought off permanently, I can at least throw some work his way, make him less of a drag in your life."

"I appreciate that, but—"

"Don't worry, Jewel. I'm not trying to get rid of Lucky. I like having him as the competition. Next to him, I look pretty good."

He flashed that expensive smile.

"It's not a competition," she said tightly.

"Everything is a competition, my dear. And there can be only one winner."

Chapter 29

Ralph Rolfe could tell something was wrong as soon as Lucky walked in the door. His friend was all slumped shoulders and shuffling feet, his freckled face creased into a frown.

"What's the matter?"

"I just had the strangest Uber ride," Lucky said. "It was unsettling."

"But everything went okay in Mexico?"

"Oh, sure." Lucky pulled a roll of bills out of the pocket of his black jeans and showed it to Ralph. "Got paid right away, too."

Lucky started to put the money back in his pocket, then caught himself.

"I guess I ought to offer you some of this money," he said. "You know, like rent or something. Help with the utilities—"

"No, no, no," Ralph interrupted. "There's no need for that. You need a place to stay. I have room. It's no big deal."

Lucky stuffed the money in the pocket, still protesting. "It's been months now."

"It's fine. Have you eaten?"

"No." Lucky put a hand over his tummy. "I'm not feeling so hot. I ate some of that Mexican bologna, and it didn't sit well."

"Have you had anything else to eat?"

"Antacids."

"That might be the problem."

"I'm starting to think there might've been something wrong with that bologna."

"Uh-oh. Think it spoiled in the heat?"

"I ate it at the beginning of the trip. It was still cold then."

"Huh. Maybe you're just not used to it. Was it spicy?"

"Kind of. It's hard to describe."

"What made you decide to sample it?"

Lucky sat beside him on the couch and told him how he chose a random roll to test. He turned it into a funny story, featuring big-eyed children watching while he lynched the bed liner and slaughtered an innocent bologna. Ralph was laughing by the time he finished.

Lucky burped into his fist. "Sure, it's funny to you. But I'm still tasting it."

"Not so tasty the second time around?"

"Tell the truth, not that tasty the first time around. I think it would be better if you fry it first."

"Like Spam."

"Yeah—"

Lucky caught himself.

"When was the last time you ate Spam?"

"I eat it once in a while," Ralph said. "Usually, it's the day before payday at the store, and Spam is all that's left in the house."

"Ah."

"It's not bad when you fry it up."

Lucky burped again. "Can we talk about something else?"

"Right. No more food."

They sat in silence for a moment, both staring at the blank TV screen, then Ralph said, "How about a beer?"

Chapter 30

When Lucky woke up around midnight, he felt like he was on fire, inside and out. He threw off the bedcovers, but that didn't help the acidic burning in his throat. He rolled out of bed, landing on his bare feet. He wore only the ancient gym shorts that passed for his pajamas, but he still felt like he was burning up. And his stomach was set on the "agitate" cycle.

"Aw, Jesus."

He made his way in the dark to the bathroom down the hall. He flipped on the light and lifted the toilet lid, ready to let the vomit fly, only to find that Ralph hadn't flushed last time he was in here. Lucky didn't want to risk a splash, so he flushed the toilet. Then he waited.

"Oh, God."

Lucky knew he was really, deeply sick when he started sounding religious.

"Sweet Lord."

He couldn't wait any longer. He crouched over the toilet and unleashed a firehose torrent of pink puke into the swirling bowl.

Then he did it again.

And again.

And one to grow on.

He felt empty, hollowed out, as he squatted over the bowl. He leaned back and hit the handle to flush the mess away.

He was covered in sweat. He yanked a purple towel off the rod and mopped his face with it.

"At least that's over."

To which his stomach replied: "Watch this."

Another wave of nausea crested in his throat and spilled into the toilet bowl. He didn't see how it was possible to puke more. He figured there was nothing left in there. But apparently, the Rojo had staying power. He coughed up another chunk of pink meat – when did he stop chewing his food properly? – and a cupful of viscous liquid that appeared to be drool.

The vomiting subsided, and Lucky spent a few minutes clearing his teeth and spitting into the toilet.

"Good God."

He flushed away the evidence, then swabbed his sweaty face with the purple towel.

"Whew."

He felt dizzy. He rested his head on his forearms, leaning against the rim of the toilet, until the smell of his own breath started to get to him.

Lucky gingerly got to his feet. His stomach quaked, but the eruptions were over for now. He washed his hands and face in the sink, managing to not look at the medicine-cabinet mirror. He was pretty sure he was an unhealthy shade of green.

He was putting toothpaste on his brush when he heard a timid knocking at the bathroom door.

"Lucky?" Ralph called from the hall. "Are you all right?"

"Do I sound all right?"

"No, not at all. You sound like you're puking up a cow."

"Sorry I woke you."

"That's okay. You need anything? Some water to drink?"

"Thanks, Ralph. I'll be okay in a minute. Go back to bed."

"You sure?"

"I'm sure."

He listened to the floorboards creak as Ralph padded away. When he was sure Ralph was back in bed, Lucky turned to the toilet.

And puked some more.

Chapter 31

Freddie Garcia didn't like having Rojo in the butcher shop overnight, especially not with Inez Montoya sniffing around the place, but he apparently had no choice. Fifteen red-wrapped rolls were still in the cooler when he got to work Friday morning.

Daniel Delgado had been distributing the bologna as fast as he received it, so they hadn't been keeping it at *El Matador*. But half of the latest load was right where they'd left it the day before, just waiting to be discovered by the snoopy meat inspector.

That kind of risk was no big deal to Delgado, Freddie thought. He's so rich that a thousand-dollar fine and some time in a courtroom wouldn't hurt him. But the rest of us would be thrown out of our jobs if the government suddenly shut down the butcher shop. Freddie couldn't afford that, not with two ex-wives. He was barely keeping up with his child-support payments now.

He looked out his office windows at the sleepy-looking butchers setting up for the day's work. The ringing of blades against sharpening steels filled the shop. Freddie's favorite song. He couldn't let Delgado's screwing around with Rojo jeopardize the mployment of those men or the loyalty of their customers.

Freddie had nearly worked himself up to phoning his boss about the Rojo when Delgado drove into the parking lot in his silver Jaguar. Freddie checked his wristwatch. He was pretty sure he'd never seen Delgado this early in the day before, ever. Maybe he was coming to take away the bologna.

Freddie neatened the papers on his desk, but he kept one eye on the window as Delgado crossed the parking lot to the front entrance. The boss was wearing a black suit with a pale blue polo shirt, his idea of casual. He smiled and waved as he walked among the employees – as usual – but Freddie thought it seemed forced.

He waved Delgado into his office before the boss could

knock.

"Good morning, Freddie. Looks like you guys are ready for business."

"Right on time. What are you doing here so early?"

"Couldn't sleep."

He sat on the wooden chair across from Freddie, who envied the drape of the expensive black suit. Most of the time, Freddie was perfectly happy in his Wranglers and boots, but sometimes he wondered what it must be like to have your clothes tailor-made.

"Got a lot on your mind?"

"Plotting and scheming." Delgado smiled. "Making big plans."

"Plans that involve the shop?"

"Bigger than that. I'm thinking a nationwide market."

Freddie got a sinking feeling. "For Rojo?"

"We're barely scratching the surface with these imports."

"Every time we make another run to the border, we're taking a big gamble."

"A small one. The only person who's likely to get into trouble is Lucky Flanagan. And he understood the risk when we started."

Delgado smiled smugly.

"What?"

"I got this image in my mind of Lucky getting strip-searched on his way into lockup. Hosed off with cold water, naked, like they do in the movies."

"What do you have against this guy?" Freddie asked. "What did he ever do to you?"

"Not a thing. I just find it amusing, how easily he can cross the border in that truck. If you tried the same thing, Immigration would ship you off to Mexico before you had a chance to prove you're an American citizen."

"Speaking of which," Freddie said, "I thought you had buyers lined up for that Rojo. It's still in the cooler."

"I'm making arrangements to take it away."

"Good. It makes me nervous, having that stuff in the cooler."

"Because of that inspector?"

"She could stop by again any time."

"If she does, we'll buy her off."

"I'm telling you, she's not the type you can buy. She's very devoted to the job."

"Ah. Our money is no good with her."

Freddie thinking: *Your* money.

"Trust me, Freddie. It'll be fine."

Chapter 32

As soon as Jewel Flanagan arrived at her office, before anyone else was there to overhear, she called Lucky.

Instead of "hello," his answer was somewhere between a gasp and a groan.

"Lucky?"

"Gah?"

"What's wrong with you?"

"I'm sick. I've been awake all night, throwing up."

"Oh, no!" Jewel was caught off-guard by the upwelling of sympathy in her chest. She kept telling herself she no longer cared for him, but her emotions often betrayed her. "Do you need a doctor?"

"It's just food poisoning, I think."

"Food poisoning can kill you."

"Not so far. But it came close."

He made a grunting, groaning noise, and her sympathy turned to disgust.

"Are you about to be sick again?"

"No, I was just sitting up. I'm still in bed."

"Sorry I woke you. You need your sleep if you're ill."

"I'm okay. Or, I will be."

"I should let you go."

"I'm awake now. What's up?"

Jewel didn't see any way to wade in slowly. She went for the plunge.

"Daniel Delgado."

"What?"

"Daniel. Delgado."

"Is that name supposed to mean something to me?"

"Doesn't it?"

He hesitated, like maybe something had clicked, but he said, "Never heard of him."

"He's my—" Oh, man, she did not want to say the word

"boyfriend." It sounded so junior high. "He's the man I've been seeing."

A long silence.

Finally, he said, "I thought you didn't want me to know anything about your new social life."

"I'm sorry, Lucky. This could wait. I didn't know you were sick—"

"No, no, go ahead. I'm fascinated."

That sarcastic edge in his voice. It had been one of the first negatives she'd discovered about him, *after* they were married. When he felt hurt or angry, he went straight to that nasty voice.

"We were at dinner last night, and he told me—"

"Wait, wait. What fancy restaurant was this? I want to picture the scene."

She sighed. "High Noon. In Old Town."

"I remember that place. Very fancy. I took you there on a date, when we were first going out."

"I remember."

"So, you're at High Noon with Mr. Daniel Delgado, having a fine meal, and he tells you, what?"

"That you're working for him."

He made that gagging sound again and she heard the bed squeak, as if he'd jumped to his feet.

"Say that again."

"You're working for him. He owns that shop where you delivered the Mexican bologna."

A pause while he absorbed what she'd said.

"First of all," he said, "let's not talk about illegal activity over the phone where anyone could be listening. And, secondly, I didn't know this guy Delgado was the boss. I reported to the butcher shop manager, a guy named Freddie. Are you dating him, too?"

Jewel's face felt instantly hot and her vision went blurry, but she kept her voice under control. Her coworkers would come through the front door any minute now, and she couldn't afford to start the workday bawling.

"I've only been seeing Daniel. And I didn't *start* seeing him until after you moved out."

"Like I believe that."

"It's the truth."

He snorted. She let it go.

"Daniel told me last night that he was the one behind hiring you for those trips to the border. I thought you should know that."

"Thanks."

"He might be crossing you up in some way."

"Like how?"

"I don't know. Just watch yourself. You don't want to take a fall for Daniel Delgado. He's not worth it."

"Ooh, I like the sound of that. Did your relationship go sour last night? Was your dinner ruined?"

That edge. She didn't need this shit.

"Once your name came up," she said, "I lost my appetite."

"Nice."

"Be careful, Lucky."

She hung up.

Chapter 33

Ralph Rolfe knew Lucky was awake. He could hear him in his room, talking on the phone. Ralph couldn't make out the words, but from the caustic tone, he'd wager Lucky was talking to Jewel.

Ralph thought about pouring Lucky a cup of coffee, but he wasn't sure coffee would be appreciated by a stomach that had been turning itself inside-out all night long. Maybe some milk?

Lucky burst out of his bedroom about then, stuffing his phone into the hip pocket of his black jeans. He wore the usual black T-shirt, but his feet were bare, and they looked super-white against the grimy hardwood floor. Lucky's face, though, was bright red.

"Oh, wait till you hear this!" he shouted. "You're not gonna believe it."

Ralph sat up straighter on the gut-sprung sofa, trying to look attentive.

"I told you Jewel was seeing some guy, right? Some rich guy?"

Ralph nodded.

"Guess who he is."

"Jeff Bezos."

"No, wait."

"Bill Gates."

"No, I didn't—"

"Bruce Wayne!"

"Stop guessing! I didn't mean for you to actually guess. I was being, you know, *rhetorical*."

Ralph thought that was a pretty big word for someone who'd just risen from a night of toilet worship, but he clammed up. Guessing was more fun, but Lucky didn't seem to have any patience this morning.

"His name is Daniel Delgado."

Ralph blinked. The name meant nothing to him.

"He's the guy who hired me to smuggle the bologna from Mexico."

"Her *boyfriend*?"

"Well, she didn't use that term, exactly—"

"I thought you were hired by a guy named Freddie."

"Delgado is Freddie's boss."

"Ah. The kingpin."

"The what?"

"Never mind."

"Jewel thinks her *boyfriend*—" The word made Lucky grimace. "—is setting me up somehow. Like, maybe he wants me to get caught at the border so I'm out of the picture."

"I thought you were already out of the picture."

"With Jewel?"

"Doesn't she keep asking you for a divorce?"

"She doesn't really mean it. She's going through a phase."

"A phase that includes dating the King of Bologna?"

Lucky sighed.

"Do you think Freddie knows about the connection?" Ralph asked. "To Jewel, I mean."

"I wondered about that. If he does, he's one helluva an actor."

"Maybe you should ask him. It might clear up some things."

Lucky studied his bare toes for a moment, then he looked at Ralph.

"Do I smell coffee?"

Chapter 34

Inez Montoya had just finished her morning cinnamon roll when her cell phone rang. She carefully set her half-full coffee cup on the dashboard and checked the readout on her phone: "Dr. M."

She winced. Dr. Mustafa Salam worked at the state Poison Control Office at the University of New Mexico Medical Sciences Center. It was part of his job to track the spread of food-borne illness. Whenever he called, it was never good news.

Inez thought "Dr. M," as everyone called him, should be called Dr. Death or Dr. Doom. Because, like a comic-book villain, the pathologist took way too much delight in the demise of others. Over the past few years, Inez had led him to believe she shared his fascination with widespread death, which meant Dr. M often called her with a heads-up before filing his official reports about deadly food.

"My dear Inez," he said when she answered. "I've got something for you. Something juicy."

She made a face, but he couldn't see. "What is it?"

"A tip from the UNM emergency room," he said. "Four cases of apparent food poisoning overnight. Reactions so severe they went to the ER. Who knows how many others are toughing it out without consulting a doctor."

"Oh, my."

"Yes. Someone has made a mistake, for sure."

"They all eat at the same place?"

"I'm told not," he said. "However, they are all Hispanic patients, and they all reported buying food from local butchers or *bodegas*."

Inez felt her pulse quicken.

"Mexican bologna?"

"I beg your pardon?"

"Do you know exactly what they ate?"

"I just record the numbers. But some of the patients are

probably still at the ER if you want to ask them yourself."

Inez cranked up her government car.

"I'm on my way."

Chapter 35

Lucky Flanagan still felt shaky as he arrived at *El Matador Carnicería*. He hadn't thrown up in a couple of hours, but he'd consumed nothing but coffee and water so far today, and his stomach gurgled as he stepped into the butcher shop's air-conditioned interior.

The display case full of raw meat made Lucky's stomach do a backflip, and he kept his black sunglasses on as he approached the counter, his gaze aimed just over the cashier's Brylcreemed head.

"Is Freddie Garcia here?"

Lucky could see from where he was standing that Freddie's glassed-in corner office was dark and empty.

"He had to step out for a minute," said the young cashier. "Anything I can help you with?"

"No, that's okay. I need to talk to Freddie."

Lucky turned away from the meat counter and wandered the few short aisles of groceries. Canned chilé peppers and bags of corn meal and dried pinto beans – the basics in New Mexico – sat among brightly packaged goods from Mexico. At least the sight of them didn't turn his stomach.

While he waited, a woman yanked open the front door and marched inside. She was Hispanic, maybe thirty years old, dressed in jeans and sandals and an old T-shirt with Disney characters on the front. She had the harried air of a full-time mom.

"I've got a complaint," she said to the same clean-cut cashier who'd tried to wait on Lucky.

"Yes, ma'am?"

She frowned at the interruption, or maybe at being called "ma'am," but she kept talking.

"I bought some Rojo from you people yesterday afternoon," she said. "Served it to my husband and my three kids last night. I won't eat that shit, but my husband grew up on it, and he thinks it's great."

The clerk's face had gone bright red.

"If you're referring to that bologna from Mexico," he said, "you must be mistaken, ma'am. We don't sell that here."

"Don't give me that. I bought it from your boss. And there was something wrong with it. My husband and my children were up all night, puking their guts out. I had to call my mother in the middle of the night to come over and help me. She's there with them now. She said I should get some rest, but I wanted to come here first and tell you idiots that you're poisoning people."

She got kind of loud toward the end, and the young clerk was wide-eyed with panic.

"I don't know what to tell you, ma'am—"

"You can't tell me anything I don't know already. My family is sick and it's because of that bologna. Tell your boss, before he gives the whole South Valley food poisoning."

She turned on her heel and strode out of the butcher shop.

The blushing clerk glanced over at Lucky, who pretended to be engrossed in the Nutrition Facts on a can of olives.

"Wow," the kid said, too loud. "That woman must be crazy."

Lucky didn't look over at him. Something else had caught his eye: A blue Chevy Impala pulling into the parking lot, Freddie Garcia behind the wheel.

Lucky put the can back on the shelf and went out the front door into the morning sunshine. He walked around the building to meet Freddie as he was getting out of his car.

"Good morning," Garcia said when he saw him.

"Not so far."

"What do you mean?"

"I was up all night, throwing up."

"Yeah, you look kinda pale." Garcia tried not to grin when he said it, but he couldn't fight it off.

Lucky frowned at him.

"I'm serious. There was something wrong with that Rojo."

Garcia shushed him with a look and jerked his head toward the back door of the butcher shop. They went inside and were seated in Garcia's office with the door closed before Garcia said, "Now, what are you talking about?"

"There was a woman in here just now who said she fed Rojo to her family and they were sick all night long."

Garcia's brow furrowed.

"She said she got the bologna here?"

"She told the kid out front that she got it from his boss. I assumed she meant you."

"Not me. I haven't sold any of it out of the shop."

Lucky thought about what Jewel had told him about Daniel Delgado being the big boss, but he wasn't ready to spring that name on Freddie yet. Not while he still felt like crap.

"*Whoever* is selling it is liable to kill somebody."

"That bad, huh?"

"I threw up, like, ten times."

"Jesus Christ. That stuff has been distributed all over town. I just took the rest of it to a buyer from Colorado."

"That's what I was afraid of," Lucky said. "I came right over—"

"Wait a minute. When did *you* eat Rojo?"

"Um, oh, I was gonna mention that. I kinda got nervous down in Juarez, thinking that maybe there was something inside those rolls. So I took one and cut it up and ate some of it—"

"The missing roll," Garcia said.

"Yeah, sorry about that."

"Was it still cold then?"

"Absolutely."

"And you drove straight back to Albuquerque?"

"Hey, don't try to pin this on me," Lucky said. "There was something wrong with that bologna when it left the factory."

Garcia rocked back in his chair, considering this. He wore his usual cowboy garb, and he steepled his fingers in front of his chin.

"It must've been an accident," he said. "We haven't done anything to cross the owners at Rojo."

"Wait a minute. You think it's possible that somebody

tainted that bologna *on purpose*?"

Garcia shook his head, but he still seemed to be weighing the possibility.

"The young guy at Rojo," Lucky said. "Marco Rivera?"

"What about him?"

"We were talking together while his two thugs loaded the Rojo on the truck."

"Thugs?"

"Silent bodybuilder types. Lots of tattoos. Marco told me he hired them right out of prison."

"Hmm."

"Marco had a big pistol stuck in his belt. Like he's expecting trouble all the time."

"What kind of trouble?"

"He said he was protecting Rojo's secret recipe. I didn't believe him, but he had that pistol, so I didn't ask more questions."

Garcia nodded.

"Marco asked me if my boss was trying to make Rojo himself."

"What?"

"Like, trying to duplicate the secret recipe."

"What did you tell him?"

"I told him we were reselling it to a few Rojo fans, and I didn't know anything about the secret recipe."

"Did that satisfy him?"

"I guess. We changed the subject. I didn't think anything about it until now."

"If Marco Rivera thought we were trying to cut him out of the picture, maybe he *did* put something in that bologna that wasn't supposed to be there."

Lucky felt queasy at the thought that he'd been deliberately poisoned. He must've blanched because Garcia said, "You'd better go outside."

"I'll be okay."

"I've got to make some calls anyway. Try to prevent this

thing from spreading further."

"Gotcha." Lucky got to his feet. He teetered there a second, finding his balance. He did not feel well. Not at all.

"Go home," Garcia said. "Go back to bed."

"But what about the—"

"I'll be in touch."

Chapter 36

Jewel Flanagan stopped by Ralph Rolfe's house during her lunch hour and found Lucky in bed. He was shivering, a blanket pulled up to his chin. His freckles stood out against his pale skin, and his red hair was greasy and stiff with sweat.

"Oh, honey, look at you," she said. "You're so sick."

He nodded feebly. "I feel like I've got the flu or something."

"You're dehydrated from all the vomiting."

"I drank some water."

"When?"

"What time is it?"

He raised up on one elbow, as if to get up from bed, but Jewel stopped him with a hand on his shoulder. He was wearing a faded black T-shirt, and his skin felt hot through the thin cotton.

"Maybe you picked up a bug down south," she said. "Time for you to rest some more."

"I've been resting. Ever since I got back from the butcher shop."

"You went there today?"

"This morning. I wanted to warn them, in case the bologna was making other people sick, too."

"You're sure it's the bologna?"

"They're getting complaints from customers."

"Oh, my. Stay right there. I'll get you some water."

She started to leave the room, but a thought stopped her. "Ralph's not here?"

"He's at work."

"The front door was standing wide open."

"Yeah, he's forgetful like that."

Jewel sighed and went into the filthy kitchen. She tried not to look at any surface too carefully, for fear that she'd see something move. She found a glass and filled it with water and hurried out of the kitchen.

Lucky was right where she'd left him, looking miserable.

"I brought this on myself," he moaned. "I shouldn't ever have eaten that bologna."

"There was no way for you to know—"

"I think the Mexicans deliberately poisoned that shipment."

"What?"

"I don't know if it was actual poison, like you read about in books. Maybe they just let the bologna spoil, then cooled it again. I don't know how that works, exactly, but it seems the Mexicans were willing to make a lot of people sick. The question is why?"

Jewel shrugged.

"I think they were sending a personal message to your boyfriend."

She stiffened at the word "boyfriend," but this was no time to have that argument.

"What kind of message?"

"I don't know," he said. "Maybe you should ask Daniel Delgado."

Chapter 37

By the time she found Mariposa Ortega sitting in a busy corridor at the University of New Mexico hospital, Inez Montoya was feeling frustrated. One of the food-poisoning victims had already gone home, and the families of the other two were cagey about what the victims had eaten, which told Inez it had been something illicit like Mexican bologna.

Now here was Mariposa, wringing her hands over her sick child, a boy of four who was on an IV because he couldn't keep down any fluids. She sat in a plastic chair at the foot of his bed, which was screened from the rest of the triage area by blue curtains.

Mariposa resembled her namesake butterfly. Beautiful, but flighty and fluttery. She'd clearly been up all night. Her makeup was smudged, and her long black hair bore rake marks from her running her hands through it. She did that now, pushing the hair back from her lovely face, and Inez felt immediately intimidated. She'd always had trouble with the pretty girls.

"I know you've had a rough night," Inez said in Spanish. "But I need your help, so we can prevent others from getting sick like your son."

Mariposa nodded, still wringing her hands.

"This sounds like a meat-borne illness," Inez said, fishing. "Did your son eat something out of the ordinary?"

Mariposa didn't hesitate.

"*Bolonía*," she said. "The Rojo brand from Mexico."

"Ah," Inez said, "I thought it might be something like that."

Mariposa's pretty face hardened.

"It's his grandfather. My father-in-law. He's always feeding stuff like that to my kid. Teaching him the 'old ways.' Now look where it's gotten us."

Inez hated to trample on that simmering anger, but the biggest question remained unasked.

"Do you know where your father-in-law got the Rojo?"

"He was bragging about it," Mariposa said, "how he had friends who could get special shipments."

"Do you know who they are?"

Mariposa looked up and down the tiled hall, making sure no one was listening.

"The Hernandez brothers at *Carne Grande*," she said. "They're from Mexico originally, same as my father-in-law. They're like a little club of people devoted to this particular bologna."

"Did your father-in-law get sick, too?"

"He's got an iron stomach from eating hot peppers his whole life. Not like a little boy—"

Mariposa's words caught in her throat, and tears filled her eyes. Inez looked away, uncomfortable with the sudden emotion.

"I'm sure he'll be fine," she said.

"The doctor says so, too. But look at him, so little in that hospital bed."

The boy, sound asleep despite the IV in his arm, was a dark-haired cherub. Even Inez, who generally avoided sticky, noisy children, could see that he was a beautiful child.

The thought that some greedy bastard had caused the boy's sickness infuriated her. She would by God track down the illegal bologna and punish those responsible.

She'd start by shutting down the Hernandez brothers.

Whether her boss liked it or not.

Chapter 38

Freddie Garcia was on his feet as soon as he saw Daniel Delgado's sleek Jaguar cruise into the parking lot. He met his boss at the back of the butcher shop, holding the door open for him as Delgado breezed into the office.

"I've been trying to call you for three hours."

"I know, Federico, I know. You've left ten messages on my voicemail."

"If you've listened to those messages, you know we've got a big problem."

Delgado shrugged. The padded shoulders of his perfectly tailored suit barely moved.

"A small problem."

"We've fielded four complaints so far," Freddie said. "All from people who got Rojo from yesterday's shipment. I've been handing out hundred-dollar bills to keep people quiet, but that won't last. Word will get out. And I'll have that meat inspector up my ass for sure."

"Maybe she'll find your backbone up there."

Freddie shut up, but he was seething on the inside.

"One bad shipment doesn't ruin everything," Delgado said. "A few people got sick, but nobody died, right?"

"As far as we know."

"I think we would've heard something by now. The question is: What happened to that bologna? Did it spoil while Lucky was driving it to Albuquerque?"

Freddie shook his head.

"Lucky says it was bad from the get-go. He ate some of it raw before he left Juarez, and it made his sick."

Delgado brightened. "Really? Lucky has been ill?"

"He came by here this morning, looking like hell. Said he'd been up all night puking."

Delgado laughed heartily. "There's a pretty picture! Almost makes it worth the trouble."

Freddie shook his head. His boss had such a strange vendetta against Lucky Flanagan. He couldn't understand it.

"Lucky said Marco Rivera was carrying a gun at the Rojo plant, and he had a couple of bad boys working for him. Marco's afraid somebody will steal the secret recipe."

"I've known Marco since college. He's always been paranoid."

"Just what we want in a business partner."

"He won't be our partner much longer," Delgado said, smiling.

"No?"

"I can't forgive him for shipping us bad bologna. We're done with him."

"Good."

"There's no sense building a market for Rojo if our supply chain can be so easily disrupted."

Freddie glowered at him. With Daniel Delgado, everything came down to a business model.

"We need our own manufacturing set-up, and we need to make it happen in a hurry to capitalize on the fad."

"And how do we get Marco to give us the secret recipe?"

Delgado gave him that mischievous smile again.

"I've been on the phone with Señor Villa, talking about that very thing. He's tired of doing business in Mexico. Things have been bad at Rojo since his partner died. He thinks Marco is a punk."

"From what I've heard, I'd have to agree with him."

"Señor Villa thinks it's time that he retired to Angel Fire. He's got a place up there in the mountains, just a cabin really, and he wants to live up there before he's too old to manage it."

Freddie did not like the sound of this.

"For the right amount of money, Señor Villa will sell us the Rojo recipe," Delgado said. "We can put it into production, and he can go enjoy his golden years."

Freddie crossed his arms over his chest and stared at his messy desk, thinking. Finally, he looked up at Delgado and said,

"Marco won't let him go. Not if he suspects anything."

"Señor Villa will simply vanish. By the time Marco figures out we're involved, it'll be too late. We'll be up and running, making American Rojo."

"That's what you're going to call it?"

"Why not? We'll put an American flag on the package to make sure people understand it's made in the good old U.S. of A. We'll appeal to their patriotism. 'Make America Fat Again.'"

He laughed at his own joke, but Freddie kept his face stony.

"The market could dry up before then. The food poisoning—"

"If anything, that will help us. We'll warn people not to eat that risky stuff from Mexico. They should eat nice, safe American Rojo instead."

He had an answer for everything. It made Freddie feel overwhelmed and sort of queasy.

"You've already got this all arranged."

"Almost all," Delgado said. "Señor Villa doesn't drive anymore because he's on some kind of heart medication. We need to send someone down to pick him up and bring him to Albuquerque."

"Don't look at me. I'm not risking my ass in Juarez."

"I didn't mean you, Freddie. You're management. That sort of work is beneath you."

Freddie could tell Delgado was yanking his chain, but he didn't rise to the taunt.

"So who does it?"

Delgado smiled. "I was thinking we'd send Lucky Flanagan."

Chapter 39

Inez Montoya's heart pounded as she climbed out of her government Ford in front of the *Carne Grande* butcher shop on Mountain Road. A couple of hipster women, all braids and bracelets and Birkenstocks, emerged from the shop, chattering with each other, not even noticing Inez standing there in her uniform. She caught the door before it could swing closed, and marched inside.

The handsome Hernandez brothers, Raul and Rick, were behind the counter, but there were no customers at the moment. That made things a little easier for Inez.

She strode up to the counter, her clipboard before her like a shield. The brothers looked at each other, then back at her, their smiles flashing uncertainly.

Inez addressed herself to Rick. "You told me you weren't selling Rojo out of your shop."

"That's right," he said cautiously.

"I just talked to a woman at the UNM emergency room. She's been there all night with her sick child. A four-year-old boy. You know why he's sick?"

She didn't give him time to answer.

"Because his grandfather fed him Rojo last night, and it was tainted or spoiled or something."

The brothers exchanged another look. No smiles now.

"What does any of this have to do with us?" Rick said.

"This mother is very angry. She happily told me Grandpa bought the bologna right here at your store."

Raul shook his head. "One person makes an accusation. That's not enough to come around here—"

"It's more than enough," Inez snapped. "Three other people were at that same ER with food poisoning. It won't take much of an investigation to track it all back to Rojo."

"You can't prove anything," Rick said.

"Federal regulations let me shut you down until the

investigation verifies that you're operating a safe and legal butcher shop."

"Aw, come on."

"See this red sticker? When I walk out that front door, I'm pasting it on the door. As you can see, it says 'Closed Until Further Notice.'"

"You'll ruin us," Raul said.

"You should've thought about that before you started dealing Mexican bologna to your friends. Now look where it's got you. Was it worth it?"

The brothers hung their heads.

Inez let the silence build for a full minute, then she said, "There is one possible way out."

They looked up at her, hope in their eyes.

"Tell me where you got the Rojo, and it can go easier on you. We'd much rather bust your supplier than close you down."

"Can't do it," Rick said. "I told you before, it's too risky. You get on the wrong side of certain people in this town—"

"You've already done much worse than that," Inez interrupted.

"What do you mean?"

"You got on the wrong side of *me*."

Chapter 40

By late Friday afternoon, Lucky Flanagan felt better, piled up on the sofa with a blanket around his shoulders, sipping hot lemon tea. He normally wouldn't touch tea, hot or otherwise, but he'd found an old box of teabags in Ralph's cabinet and the label said it was supposed to be "soothing."

The big TV silently showed some random documentary about wild animals in Africa, and Lucky watched as a leopard dashed out of the tall grass and took down a thrashing gazelle. Within seconds, the perky gazelle was turned into a bloody lunch.

"At least I'm having a better day than that." Lucky belched loudly and added, "Just barely."

The doorbell rang, and he called out, "Come in!" He figured it was Jewel, coming by to check on him on her way home from work. So he was surprised when Freddie Garcia clumped into the dim living room.

Garcia was dressed in boots, Wranglers and cowboy shirt, as usual, and the front of his shirt was damp with sweat, a sort of Rorschach butterfly on his chest. He stopped just inside the door, his fists on hips, looking around the cluttered living room with distaste.

"Oh, hey," Lucky said as he tried to sit up straighter on the squishy sofa. "I wasn't expecting company."

Garcia looked him over and said, "You look like shit."

"Thanks."

"Feeling any better?"

"I'm on the mend. I'll be back to normal in two, three years. Why?"

"You up to another run to Juarez? Tomorrow?"

Lucky shook his head, which made him feel woozy.

"No more bologna runs for me," he said. "I feel terrible that we gave food poisoning to people. That's why I'm so sick: I'm being punished."

Garcia shook his head, a sour look on his dark face.

"You're sick because you didn't trust us," he said. "You thought we were trying to put something over on you, so you gobbled up a bunch of product and told me there was a miscount."

Lucky hung his head. Not from shame, but from illness. He felt like Garcia's stern voice was bouncing off his skull. That tea wasn't soothing a damned thing.

He unleashed a mighty lemon-flavored burp, but it didn't seem to help. Garcia made a face at his manners.

"Sorry," Lucky said. "Today, there's no telling what might come out of my mouth. I'm ready to call an exorcist."

Garcia took a step backward, so he was standing closer to the door.

"All you've got to do tomorrow is drive," he said. "Down to Juarez and back. No bologna involved. You won't even need the truck. You can use your own car."

"What would I be bringing back, if not bologna?"

"A person."

"Oh, no. I'm not smuggling illegal immigrants into the country for you. In fact, I'm not even—"

"The man's got his immigration papers in order, numb-nuts. He's just too old to drive."

"I don't care," Lucky said. "No more Mexico for me."

"You even know the guy. Your pal José Villa."

That pulled Lucky up short.

"Señor Villa's coming north?"

"He's going into retirement," Garcia said. "He's got a place in the mountains up by the Colorado border. But you'd just bring him back here to Albuquerque. We'll take care of the rest."

"You don't have somebody else who could drive down to Juarez? One of your butchers? Somebody who hasn't been up all night puking?"

"The boss wants you to do it," Freddie said. "He trusts you."

Lucky sat up straighter. Anger burned in his churning belly.

"I know who your boss is," he snapped. "Daniel Delgado.

He's trying to screw me over, isn't he?"

"I don't know what you mean."

"He's banging my wife," Lucky said. "I mean, we're separated, so it's more like she's my ex-wife, but there's still a chance we could get back together. But not while your boss is squiring her around town in his Jaguar."

Garcia's eyes widened, as if the connection to Jewel was news to him, but Lucky remained on guard.

"Delgado wants me to fail. He'd love to see me in a Mexican jail."

"It's not like that," Garcia said. "He simply wants Villa up here. They've got business to do together before the old man goes into retirement."

"What kind of business?"

"You don't need to know that. You're just the driver."

"I'm not doing it," Lucky said.

"I'll give you a thousand dollars."

Lucky had opened his mouth to say something else, and his face froze that way while he considered what Garcia had offered. He snapped out of it and said, "Two thousand."

"All right."

"That was too easy," Lucky said. "I should've said three thousand."

"Don't push it," Freddie said. "This is an easy job. For three thousand, I'd do it myself."

"Where do I find him?"

Freddie fished a folded piece of yellow paper out of his shirt pocket and tossed it onto the coffee table.

"That's his address. He'll be waiting for you."

"Will he be alone?"

"He sure as hell better be. If you see Marco or his thugs, haul ass out of there and try again later."

"Marco knows about this?"

"Don't worry about Marco. I'm just saying to watch yourself down there, as always."

Lucky nodded, but he was lost in thought, trying to figure

out exactly what Daniel Delgado had in mind. He remembered the leopard kill on the TV. In this scenario, Lucky was pretty sure he was the gazelle.

"See you tomorrow," Garcia said, and he went out the door, leaving Lucky to his fears and doubts.

Chapter 41

Jewel Flanagan watched through her cracked front window as Daniel Delgado's silver Jaguar purred into her driveway. She remembered the first few times he'd picked her up in that car; she could practically *hear* the neighbors speculating about how Jewel was coming up in the world. Now, the sleek sedan just looked out of place in her dusty neighborhood.

She met him at the front stoop, pushing open the screen to lean in the doorway, her arms crossed over her chest. She was in full Mom mode – her hair was pulled back into a ponytail and she was dressed in cutoffs and an old football jersey – and Daniel gaped at her for a moment before he caught himself.

"I thought we had a dinner date," he said. "You're not ready?"

"I'm not going."

"Are you sick?"

"No. I'm just not going out with you anymore. I wanted to tell you face to face. We're finished."

"What?" His eyes widened. "Why?"

Jewel clamped her lips shut before any words could escape. She shook her head. She didn't owe him an explanation.

"Is it because of Lucky? Are you still hung up on him?"

She shook her head again, though she'd been asking herself that same question all day.

"It's not about that," she said. "But now that you've brought it up, I don't like the way you've been using him. Putting him in danger. For what? Bologna!"

Daniel's face had slipped into that easy smile, the one that said he found the whole world slightly amusing.

"I threw some work his way," he said. "He needed the money, or he wouldn't have taken the job."

"Yes, but—"

"He didn't suffer any harm."

"He was sick all night—"

"He didn't *die*. Other people got sick off that shipment, too, but nobody was permanently injured."

"That's not the point—"

"At least he got paid for his puking."

He was smiling again, smug. Jewel felt an emotional shift, as if she'd suddenly seen through him. How could she ever have been attracted to such a petty man?

"Not everything is about money."

He shrugged. "Not everything. But most things."

"I don't see it that way. I think people have value."

"Even losers like Lucky?"

"Especially Lucky. You know why he's done these smuggling runs? To impress me. He's called me from the road, letting me know he's okay and telling me about his trip, like it's some great adventure."

"He's got a low threshold for excitement," Daniel said.

"It's not that he was excited. He wanted *me* to be excited. He's all like, 'See, Jewel? I can do something on my own. I can make some money.' And the whole time you're playing puppet-master, pulling his strings, making him jump and dance. It's pitiful."

Daniel glanced over his shoulder, as if he'd heard his Jaguar calling.

"Is that what you're looking for in a man, Jewel? Somebody you can pity?"

"Of course not—"

"Because if that's case, I'm definitely not the man for you."

Jewel stopped herself before she could defend Lucky again. Instead, she said, "Let's just leave it right there. Thanks for all the dinners and dates. Best of luck to you."

She let the screen door close and stepped back so she could close the wooden front door, too. Daniel hadn't moved.

"Luck?" he sneered. "I don't need luck. Things don't happen to me, Jewel. I *make* things happen."

She shut the door.

Chapter 42

When Ralph Rolfe got home from work at the comic book store, he found Lucky on the couch, wrapped in a grungy blanket, his red hair sticking up in all directions like a feather duster.

"Still sick?"

Lucky shook his head. "I'm on the mend."

"Good," Ralph said. "Want a beer?"

"God, no. I'll take some more of that lemon tea, if you don't mind making it."

"Coming right up!"

Ralph bustled off to the kitchen and set the kettle on the stove and got himself a Blue Moon beer, which tastes like oranges and makes for some fruity burping. Soon as the tea was ready, he took the steaming cup into the living room and carefully handed it to Lucky.

"Thanks, Ralph."

"Happy to help." For Ralph, that was really true. It wasn't often that he found himself in the position of being able to help Lucky (if you didn't count the whole free rent deal), and it made him happy to fetch his sick friend some tea.

Ralph flopped onto the sofa, which made Lucky hold his teacup high and say, "Whoa!" But none of the tea spilled, and Ralph sat still as he asked Lucky if he'd eaten anything.

"Not yet. But soon."

"I can make you some toast."

"Maybe. I've got to get back to normal. I'm driving down to Juarez again tomorrow."

"Oh, no, Lucky. You're not doing another bologna run. Haven't you learned anything from—"

"Not bologna. A man."

Ralph clapped his hand over his mouth.

"It's okay," Lucky said. "He's not illegal or anything. He just needs a ride to Albuquerque."

"But it's for those same people, the bologna smugglers?"

"You don't want to know the details. Let's just say I'm about to come into some real money. It'll be worth the trip."

"I don't like it, Lucky. You already got sick once. Maybe next time you don't get well."

"It's not like that. No bologna. No food products at all. Just a guy who needs a ride."

Lucky sipped his hot tea.

"Who is this guy?" Ralph asked. "Do you know him?"

"We've met. I think I told you about him. Señor Villa, the old guy at the bologna factory."

"The one who knows the secret recipe!"

"That's right. He's coming up to New Mexico to retire."

"And he's paying you to drive him?"

"Well, not exactly. Daniel Delgado is paying me."

"Can you trust that guy, Lucky? Can you trust any of those guys? Maybe you're their sacrificial goat."

"Their what?"

"Sacrificial goat."

"I'm not any kind of goat."

"You know what I mean."

"No, I do not."

"Natives stake a goat outside the village to attract the lion at night. Better that they lose a goat than have a lion come into camp."

"This is, like, in Africa?"

"Yeah. But it's anywhere really. It's a metaphor."

"I have no idea what you're talking about. I must be having a relapse."

"Delgado and his people," Ralph insisted. "They're happy to sacrifice you if it gets them what they want."

"Nah, it's not like that."

"Are you sure?"

Lucky shrugged.

"They're offering me two grand to go get Señor Villa. I can't turn down that money. I need the capital so I can start a business of my own. And Scarlett's birthday is coming up."

Ralph stared at the blank TV screen. He could see their reflections in the screen – vague, lumpy shapes on the gut-sprung sofa. He tugged at the front of his Captain America shirt, making sure his belly was covered.

"Why so much?" he asked.

"What?"

"Why are they willing to pay you so much to drive this guy up from Mexico?"

"I negotiated a good deal."

"It's got to be dangerous in some way," Ralph said. "Otherwise, they would've offered you the usual five hundred."

"I wouldn't have done it for five hundred. I told Freddie as much. He offered a thousand, but I talked him to up to two."

They sat in silence. Ralph felt like machinery was turning inside his head, the meshing gears finally spitting out an idea.

"You think the Rojo guys are going to let Villa leave with you?"

"Sure, why not?"

"He knows the secret recipe."

"So what? He's retiring."

"If I were them," Ralph said, "I wouldn't let him leave Mexico alive."

Chapter 43

By Saturday morning, Lucky Flanagan felt better. He'd slept hard, catching up after the gastronomical nightmare of the night before, and he felt clear-headed and steady. He even managed to eat some toast with his coffee and keep it all down.

He was on the road before the sun cleared the Sandias, headed south on Interstate 25. The sooner he completed this mission, the better.

Lucky had to concede that Ralph was probably right about Daniel Delgado and Freddie Garcia. They no doubt considered him an expendable gringo, the sacrificial goat. If things went wrong today, he couldn't count on them to help.

Even if it all went perfectly, Lucky intended to keep his distance after he got his money. He had a bad feeling that Señor Villa's emigration might set off some sort of international bologna war. He didn't want to get caught in the middle.

He was south of Socorro when his cell phone rang. He expected it to be Freddie Garcia, checking up on him, but the readout said, "Jewel."

"Good morning," he said brightly.

"How are you feeling?"

"Much better. I got a good night's sleep."

"That's good. I'm glad you're going to be all right."

Something funny in her voice.

"Are *you* all right?" he asked. "Is everything okay with Scarlett?"

"She's fine. I'm fine. I just didn't get much sleep last night."

"Worrying?"

Lucky used his turn signal as he passed a slow-moving tractor-trailer truck. He gave the semi plenty of room.

"Not worrying, exactly," she said. "Wondering if I did the right thing."

That got Lucky's attention. Did she mean splitting up with him? Did she suddenly have doubts? Before he could ask, she said, "I broke up with Daniel last night. I won't be seeing him anymore."

"Whoa," Lucky blurted. "I didn't see that coming."

"It wasn't a good fit. We don't have the same values."

Lucky had no idea what she meant by that, but it didn't matter. She'd broken up with the rich guy. Which, in Lucky's mind, meant he was back in the running. His heart pounded as he checked his mirrors and returned to the slow lane.

"I have to admit, I'm happy you dumped him."

"He's a shark," she said. "He uses people. He was using you in that bologna smuggling. I'm so glad you're finished with that."

"Um."

"What? You *are* finished with Daniel Delgado, right?"

"Mostly."

"What does that mean, Lucky?"

"One last run," he said. "But no bologna. Nothing illegal. I'm just driving a guy from Juarez to Albuquerque."

"For Daniel."

"Well, for Freddie Garcia. Who works for Daniel Delgado. It's all part of the same—"

"I can't believe it. Don't you ever learn your lesson?"

"What do you mean?"

"Daniel keeps sending you down there because it's dangerous. It's like a game to him. He *wants* something bad to happen to you."

"Nothing's gonna happen to me. I'm extra cautious where he's involved."

"Tell that to your porcelain god."

"It wasn't Delgado's fault that the bologna was tainted."

"You sure about that?"

That gave Lucky pause. He'd been willing to believe that the Mexicans would send food-poisoning to Delgado's customers, but would Delgado risk people's lives just to make Lucky sick? That didn't even make sense. Delgado had no way to know that Lucky would eat the Rojo—

"Hello?" Jewel said. "Are you still there?"

"Sorry, I got distracted, thinking about bad bologna."

"Call Daniel," she said. "Tell him the deal's off. That you don't want to go to Mexico anymore."

"I, uh, I'm driving there now, Jewel."

"What?"

"It's kinda too late to back out."

"No, it's not. Turn around and come back to Albuquerque."

"They promised me two thousand dollars. For one day's work! I'll drive this guy to Albuquerque, then I'll never do business with Daniel Delgado again."

He waited for an answer, but none came.

"Jewel?"

Nothing. She'd hung up on him.

Chapter 44

Inez Montoya stormed into *El Matador Carnicería*, clipboard in hand, and made a beeline for Freddie Garcia's office in the back. One of the beefy butchers took a step toward her, as if to block her way, but he got a look at the fire in her eyes and went right back to work.

Inez knocked on Garcia's office door but didn't wait for an invitation. She stepped into his messy office and closed the door behind her.

"Ah, the lovely and talented Inspector Montoya," Garcia said, a big fake smile under his thin mustache. "Working on a Saturday?"

"Mock me all you like," she said, "but things have changed now. The shoe is on the other horse."

"What?"

"I told you when I was here before, if I found out you were dealing in Rojo, I'd shut you down."

His eyes widened.

"We don't deal in that stuff. We never have."

"Maybe not at the retail level," she said. "But you're wholesaling it to other butcher shops around town."

Garcia's dark face lost its friendliness.

"I don't like being called a liar."

"Then stop lying," she said. "I know the Rojo came through this shop. Maybe it didn't even slow down here, but you're the pipeline."

Garcia leaned back in his swivel chair and smoothed the front of his brown Western-style shirt. He hadn't offered Inez a seat, and she didn't want one. She was too hopping mad to sit.

"You've got some evidence of this?" he asked.

"You bet I do."

"I'd like to hear that."

"Fine. Let me start with the people who went to emergency rooms all over town last night, deathly sick with food poisoning.

I talked to several of them about what they'd eaten. Evidence points to Mexican bologna as the cause."

Garcia grunted.

"We've put out the word about the tainted Rojo," she said, "but more people will eat it and will end up in the hospital. I'm sure they'll be more than happy to testify about where they purchased it."

Garcia still didn't answer.

Pen poised over her clipboard, she said, "One victim told me the bologna came from your friends over at *Carne Grande*."

"They're not my friends," Garcia said. "I barely know those guys."

"But you've met them, right? Rick and Raul Hernandez? Such nice boys."

Garcia smiled before he caught himself.

"I closed their shop down yesterday," Inez said.

"Really? For how long?"

"However long it takes to complete my investigation. I'm willing to do the same thing to you."

No smiles now. Garcia studied her a moment, and Inez thought she felt the eye of a butcher, sizing her up for dismemberment. It gave her a chill.

"I still haven't heard any actual evidence against my shop."

"I tried to get Rick and Raul to tell me where they got the Rojo, but they wouldn't talk. Not then anyway."

Garcia said nothing.

"Rick still won't talk to me," she said, "but Raul? He's a different story. He just bought a five-bedroom house in Rio Rancho. Big mortgage payment every month. He can't afford for the shop to stay closed. He called me today and told me the Rojo came from here."

"He'll say anything to get off the hook," Garcia said. "You can't believe him."

"But I do," she said. "And I'm happy to shut you down while the investigation continues."

She turned and looked through the tall windows at the

butchers working in the shop.

"You want to lose those good employees?" she said. "The minute you can't keep them on the payroll, they're gone forever."

She turned back to Garcia and found him staring at the papers strewn on the top of his desk. She'd hit a nerve.

"I might know something about this," he said finally. "Might even be willing to tell you about it, but only if my shop stays open."

"How can I guarantee that when you've probably got a cooler full of tainted Rojo right now?"

"I promise you, we don't have any."

Inez stared at him, but he waited her out.

"Fine," she said finally, "I'm not closing you down. Not today. But you'd better hold up your end of the deal."

Garcia pointed at a wooden chair across from him, and Inez finally sat. He rested his elbows on the desk and leaned toward her conspiratorially.

"There's a circle of people here in Albuquerque who are into that bologna. They're willing to pay stupid prices to get their hands on it."

She nodded, remembering what Mariposa Ortega had told her at the hospital about her father-in-law.

"I don't deal in Rojo," Garcia said. "I've always figured it wasn't worth the risk. But customers ask for it, you know? When they do, I usually send them to see Rick and Raul."

"That doesn't tell me where *they* get it from."

"I'm getting to that," he said. "There's a gringo here in a town, kind of a scumbag, who's making trips back and forth to Mexico, supplying everybody. That's the guy you're after."

"Does he have a name?"

Garcia's face cracked into a smile again, but his eyes looked hard. Somehow, that made her more inclined to believe him.

"I don't know his real name," he said. "But he goes by Lucky Flanagan."

Chapter 45

By the time Lucky found Señor Villa's hacienda, he'd persuaded himself that this whole Mexico trip was a trap masterminded by Daniel Delgado.

Delgado wanted him out of the way, everybody said so, and the fact that Jewel had spurned the rich bastard the night before didn't necessarily mean that had changed. What would make Daniel Delgado happier at this point than Lucky's arrest?

Oh, maybe my death, Lucky thought. *Especially if it happened in a sudden, gruesome way. Always possible along the border.*

Lucky navigated the streets of Ciudad Juarez much easier than he'd expected. Señor Villa lived in a residential area just off a major artery, so Lucky pretty much drove directly there. As he got close, he dialed a number on his cell phone, as his directions instructed. He switched off after the phone began to ring.

The neighborhood was swankier than Lucky had expected. All the houses were done in a Mediterranean style, two stories tall, with wrought-iron balconies and red tile roofs. Each had a perfect square of green grass out front, like a welcome mat made of irrigated sod.

Lucky went a couple of blocks into the neighborhood before he spotted Señor Villa waiting for him at the curb. The old man had two large blue suitcases sitting beside him on the concrete driveway. He wore sunglasses and baggy khaki pants and a white guayabera shirt that was damp with perspiration.

"Where have you been?" Señor Villa demanded as Lucky got out of the car. "I've been waiting here in the sun."

"The signal was that I was on my way. Not that I was waiting outside."

The old man grumbled as he opened the passenger door. "Put those bags in the trunk."

Lucky didn't remember signing on for luggage lifting, and Villa hadn't said "please," but it wasn't as if he would've stood by anyway, watching the seventy-five-year-old man heave his luggage into the back of the Mustang. Lucky hefted the heavy bags into the trunk. They barely fit, and he closed the lid on them gently.

As he got behind the wheel, he said, "Anything in those bags besides clothes and shoes and stuff? Anything that won't stand up to a search at the border?"

Señor Villa snorted. "What am I? An idiot? I know what's not allowed to cross the river. I wouldn't mess us up that way."

"I'm just being extra cautious. You've got all your papers, too, right?"

Villa rolled his eyes, but he pulled a folded sheaf of documents from his shirt pocket and held it up for Lucky to see.

"Don't worry about me, buddy boy," Villa said in his accented English. "I know what I'm doing. Do you?"

Lucky put the car in gear.

"Last chance," he said. "Forgetting anything?"

"Would you fucking go already?"

Lucky went, barely pausing at the stop sign before the Mustang galloped onto the main road. Within seconds, he was zipping along at the speed limit, checking his mirrors, watching for trouble.

"Why are you so nervous?" Villa said.

"I'm not nervous."

"You seem nervous to me. Are you afraid to cross the border?"

"I do it all the time," Lucky said. "But usually without a passenger."

"They'll ask me questions, but I've been through it before. All my papers are up to date."

"Good, good," Lucky said. "Still, I was thinking you might walk across the bridge while I bring the car over."

"*Walk*? In this heat?"

"You know how it is at the downtown bridge. The pedestrians make it across faster than the cars."

"Then what? Wait in the heat for you?"

"By the time you clear Customs, I'll be waiting for you."

Señor Villa said several things in Spanish which Lucky didn't understand. From the tone, Lucky guessed he was being cussed out. Somehow, he didn't mind it so much since it was in a foreign language on foreign soil.

When the old man paused to catch his breath, Lucky said, "We'll have you in Albuquerque before you know it."

Chapter 46

Marco Rivera felt hot all over. He hung up the phone and jumped up from his chair. He paused just a moment to stuff his pistol in his belt, then stormed out of his office in search of the Badass Brothers.

He found them outside the packing plant, shirtless and sweaty. They'd leaned a wooden pallet against the concrete-block wall and were taking turns throwing knives at it. The pocket knives were unbalanced flip-blades, all the weight in the hinge, but they still were sticking in the wood every time. Clearly, the tattooed brothers had been practicing.

They both looked at him, their eyes narrow and suspicious, the way they looked at everybody.

"The motherfucker is making a run for the border," he said in Spanish.

They showed no sign of understanding.

"Villa! He's taking off to the United States. His housekeeper just called me. She said a gringo in a blue car picked up the old man a few minutes ago. Villa took two suitcases with him. And he paid her for the whole month."

He watched the brothers process this information. He worried for a second that he'd overloaded their tiny brains, but the taller one, Tino, said, "You don't want him to go to *El Norte*."

"That's right. He knows the secret recipe for Rojo."

Blink, blink.

"He'll sell the recipe to the Americans," Marco shouted. "They'll make their own Rojo and put us out of business."

That seemed to get through their thick heads. These two idiots valued their jobs. Working for Marco was the first more-or-less straight job either had ever had, and a big step up from a Mexican prison.

"You want us to go get him," the shorter brother, Tito, said.

"That's right! Why are you standing there? See if you can catch them at the border crossing. If not, follow them over the river. He'll be going to Albuquerque, but you can catch him on the way."

"Why Albuquerque?"

"Because that's where Daniel Delgado lives. He's the one who wants to put us out of business."

"You want us to kill this Delgado?" Tito asked.

"No." Marco paused. "But if you do cross paths with him, put a blade in his ribs and tell him it's from me."

"What about Villa? Dead?"

Marco nodded. "I've warned him against selling that recipe. He knew the consequences."

The brothers clearly didn't track that last part, but it didn't matter. They had their instructions. They pulled their knives from the pallet and folded them up and put them in their hip pockets. They picked up their tank tops and slipped them on, their movements nearly identical. Marco felt like he was seeing double.

"Keep me posted," he said.

The Badass Brothers hustled over to their open Jeep and jumped into the bucket seats, buckling up as they roared into the busy street beyond the wall.

Marco stood in the parking lot for a minute, sweating under the scorching sun, after the brown Jeep had vanished from sight.

He almost wished he'd gone with them. José Villa had been part of Marco's life as far back as he could remember. He would've liked to finish Uncle José himself, but it's important for the big boss to delegate the dirty work.

He spat on the sizzling asphalt, then turned to go back inside the air-conditioned building. A spring in his step.

Chapter 47

José Villa was not a happy passenger. He stiffened up in traffic, flinching at close calls, stomping the floorboard in search of a brake pedal. The Mustang weaved in and out of the creeping traffic as it approached the border bridge, and José kept bracing for the crunch of a collision. It was almost a relief when the redhead pulled over to the curb and stopped.

"You can walk from here."

"You're serious?"

The wide, fence-lined sidewalk swarmed with people from both sides of the border, crossing over to shop or work. They looked hot and sweaty, some of the women fanning themselves. José did not want to get out in that heat.

"Just drive across," he said. "My papers are fine."

"So you say. But I'd be happier if you met me on the other side."

José stared at Lucky Flanagan for a long time, but he couldn't see the redhead's eyes behind the black sunglasses he wore. Finally, with a sigh, José popped open the door and creakily climbed out.

The heat slapped him in the face and cooked his bald head. José cursed and slammed the car door. Pedestrians near him swerved away, giving him room. He turned and joined their ranks, marching over the arching bridge toward the skyscrapers of El Paso.

He muttered under his breath that the gringo was an idiot and a bastard and a worthless criminal. But that didn't make the walk any shorter.

The crowd slowed and thickened as it reached the downhill slope of the bridge. People arranged themselves into rows, lining up for the inspection stations. At least forty people stood in front of José, going one at a time through a turnstile as they were cleared.

As he waited, he looked back at the auto traffic, trying to

pick the blue Mustang out of the dozens of cars and trucks. He couldn't see it, which didn't make him feel any better. His suitcases were in the trunk of that car.

It wasn't often that José Villa found himself among a cross-section of people. Mexicans in his economic bracket socialized only with each other. The rest they saw from the windows of air-conditioned sedans. The people in line with him looked poor and threadbare, though most of them seemed happy enough, chattering about their families or their jobs or the shopping malls across the border.

Nobody tried to talk to José. He kept his chin high and his shoulders square as he shuffled forward with the overworked *mamacitas* and the muscled-up *cholos* and the giggling girls in their heels and hoop earrings. In a crowd this lively, an old man like José was practically invisible.

When he finally reached the khaki-uniformed border inspector, José had his papers in his hand, unfolded and ready to go. The inspector was a broad-shouldered *yanqui* with a sunburned face and freckled hands. He shuffled through the papers as he said, "Just coming over for the day?"

"I've got a business meeting in El Paso," José said confidently.

"On a Saturday?"

The inspector looked José up and down, but in stifling El Paso, a crisp guayabera shirt is perfectly acceptable business attire. The *yanqui*'s gaze rested for a moment on José's gold wristwatch, then he handed back his papers and waved him through the gate.

"Have a nice day, sir."

"You, too, young man."

José ambled away from the inspection station, right in the center of the broad sidewalk that led into the United States. Once clear of the chattering crowd, José positioned himself in a stripe of shade provided by a light pole. He stood with his hands in his pockets, watching for Lucky.

The blue Mustang appeared a few minutes later, angling

across two lanes of traffic to reach him at the curb. As soon as the low-roofed car stopped, José ducked inside and off they sped in air-conditioned comfort.

Now that Lucky was safely in his home country, he seemed to relax behind the wheel, changing lanes and muscling his way through traffic with confidence. José wished he felt the same way as he stomped the empty floorboard.

"No problems?" Lucky asked.

"None. Except I sweated through my clothes."

"All smooth for me, too," Lucky said. "The inspector looked in the trunk, but he didn't even open your bags."

"Good thing," José said. "Those suitcases are full of machine guns."

The Mustang swerved as Lucky involuntarily hit the brakes. Horns honked all around them.

"*Madre mio*, get a grip on yourself," José growled. "It was a small joke."

Lucky laughed uncertainly. "I've heard funnier jokes."

"I've seen better driving."

They fell silent as Lucky changed lanes again, headed for a ramp onto the busy freeway. The urban sprawl stretched in all directions around the dry peaks of the Franklin Mountains. Much of El Paso looked just like Ciudad Juarez: humble houses with flat roofs and gravel yards and satellite dishes. But there also were the downtown office spires and the endless shopping and the imposing university and the shady haciendas along the Rio Grande. Enough to make this arid sprawl seem like a desirable step up from its neighbor across the river. No wonder so many people crossed over into the United States and never went back.

And now here was José Villa, wealthy creator of everyone's favorite bologna, doing the same thing. Slipping into the United States with the intention of never going home again.

He'd been planning this retirement for a long time, but the whole thing still seemed slightly unreal – the nervous redheaded driver, the faded old car, the business deal awaiting in Albuquerque. José felt one step removed, as if he were watching himself on TV.

"How long until we get to Albuquerque?"

"Four hours or so," Lucky said, "assuming nothing goes wrong at the inland Border Patrol station. That's about thirty minutes up the road."

"You gonna make me get out of the car again?"

"What? No, it's not like that—"

"Good," José said. "I'm finally starting to cool off. Any more time in the sun, and I'd need a shower."

"It's a drive-through thing. They'll probably just wave us through."

José thought that would be ideal. The redhead seemed to tense up at the thought of the inspection station ahead. The less he had to say or do there, in the presence of the authorities, the better.

"Maybe you'd better let me do the talking," José said.

"It'll be fine," Lucky said. "Don't worry."

José winced. Anytime somebody told him not to worry, things usually went terribly wrong.

Chapter 48

As they approached the inspection station on the way into El Paso, Tino Barreras hissed at his brother to sit down. Tito stood in the open Jeep, holding onto the roll bar, so he could get a better view of the stop-and-go traffic. They'd seen a lot of blue cars as they inched along the bridge over the Rio Grande, but not one that carried José Villa.

Tito dropped into the passenger seat, exasperated.

"Put on your seat belt," Tino said. "We don't want to give them any reason to stop us."

Tino often adopted a parental tone with his younger brother, who went through life brash and angry, a hothead. Tito needed someone to cool him down, and only his older brother could do the job. Anyone else who tried met with violent resistance.

Which made the approaching inspection station a little sketchy for the Badass Brothers. If the officers gave them any guff, Tito would likely go off on them, which would be a disaster for everyone.

"Play it cool," Tino said. "Don't say anything unless you're asked a direct question."

Tito nodded, but Tino could see the muscle twitching in his younger brother's jaw. He was clenching his teeth, grinding them together. Never a good sign.

"I mean it. Stay cool."

As the sedan ahead of them reached the inspection booth, Tino got a good look at the uniformed officer who would assess their entry into the United States. He was an older man with a droopy black mustache and silver streaks in his thinning hair. He looked sort of unhealthy, his sallow complexion blending into his saggy khaki uniform. A man counting the days to retirement.

Perfect, really, for their needs.

The sedan got the go-ahead to drive away, and Tino eased the Jeep forward to take its place. He and Tito stared at the officer, giving him their unblinking prison-yard faces. The older man looked them over, focusing on their bulked-up arms, as if reading their tattoos in search of answers. The multitude of tats seemed to make the officer nervous.

"*Buenos dias*," he said. "Papers, please."

The brothers handed over the passports that Marco Rivera had procured for them months before. The inspector flipped through them, checking the photos against their hard faces.

He met Tino's eyes as he handed back the passports, "Business or pleasure today, gentlemen?"

"Pleasure," Tito said. "We're going shopping."

"Is that so? Shopping for what?"

Tino felt Tito stiffen beside him. One question too many.

Before his brother could blurt anything, Tino said, "Shirts."

The inspector smiled, but it didn't stick. His mustache drooped over his mouth again, and he sighed.

Tino could tell he was thinking, was it worth it to search these tattooed bad boys? To refuse them admission to the United States? To hassle them in any way? Did he want to risk making such enemies? Wouldn't it be easier to wave them through?

Exactly the thoughts Tino wanted him to have.

After a moment, the older man shrugged. He stepped back from the Jeep and pointed toward El Paso.

"*Bienvenidos*," he said.

Chapter 49

Lucky Flanagan wiped the perspiration from his forehead as he approached the Border Patrol's tin-roofed inspection shed. No reason for an attack of the nerves now. The worst was over. But tell that to his sweat glands.

No lines as they approached the inspectors. Lucky hesitated, looking from one lane to another, but the decision was made for him. One of the uniformed inspectors stepped out of the shade and waved him into a stall.

"This one looks all right," Lucky said to José Villa. "But don't give him any reason to ask more questions."

"I know how to do this," the old man said. "I was crossing the border before you were born—"

"Just say as little as possible, okay?"

Señor Villa's mouth curved into a pout. He clearly wasn't accustomed to people telling him to hush. Lucky thinking: *Welcome to the United States of America, where everybody's free to tell you to shut up.*

As the Mustang crept into the shade, Lucky rolled down his window for the inspector, whose name badge said "SMITH." Lucky was beginning to think these badges weren't even their real names, like they had a bucket of generic name tags and each inspector just grabbed one at random each day—

"Sir?"

Lucky realized that Officer Smith must've said something that he'd missed.

"I'm sorry, what?"

"Your driver's license?"

"Oh, right. Sorry. You caught me daydreaming."

Señor Villa snorted.

Lucky handed the officer his license. Smith looked it over, then handed it back. He leaned down to say to Señor Villa, "Now yours."

Villa passed his papers across to the inspector, who went

through them much slower than he had the familiar American documents.

"You entering the country for business or pleasure?" Smith asked.

"Business."

Lucky thinking: *Wrong answer, knucklehead! It just leads to more questions*.

"What kind of business are you in?"

"Meat packing."

"Is that right? My dad was a butcher."

"A respectable occupation," Villa intoned, and they both nodded. Caught between them, Lucky nodded, too, though his personal experience with butchers hadn't been so respectable so far.

"I started out as a butcher," Villa said, "but I was better in the kitchen, cooking up new products."

"Really?"

Inside Lucky's head, one phrase kept repeating: *Shut up, shut up, shut up, shut up.*

"Oh, yes," Villa said, "have you heard of the Rojo brand?"

Lucky thinking: *Oh, my God, don't go there*.

The inspector lifted his sunglasses to get a better look at the old man.

"*You're* Rojo?"

"I'm the '*jo*' half. My partner was the other."

"I grew up eating that bologna," Smith said. "In El Paso. My dad always said it was something special."

"I like to think so," Villa said.

Officer Smith handed the papers back, and Lucky passed them over to Señor Villa.

"What kind of business would Mr. Rojo have in the United States?" Smith asked. He said it off-handedly, but Lucky tensed all over.

"I can't tell you." Villa winked at him. "It's top secret."

Lucky felt like pissing himself, but Officer Smith laughed.

"Good enough," he said. "I'll tell my dad I met you. And that you were on a top-secret mission."

Señor Villa cackled. Lucky wanted to pinch him.

Smith paused, like he just had a thought. "You don't have any of that bologna in the car, do you?"

"No, sir!" Lucky said before Villa could wise off.

"Then you're good to go."

As soon as Smith stepped back from the window, Lucky gave the Mustang some gas. Villa turned in his bucket seat to wave at Smith through the back window.

"What the fuck is wrong with you?" Lucky said under his breath.

"What do you mean?"

"Why did you tell that cop about Rojo? I told you to say as little as possible."

"You heard him," Villa said. "My bologna is famous. Why not mention it?"

"Because it's a good way to get searched, that's why."

"So what? We *don't* have any Rojo in the car. Let 'em search."

"My instructions were to bring you to Albuquerque without making a lot of noise."

"Who's making noise?"

Chapter 50

Inez Montoya parked in front of a ranch-style house in a subdivision on Albuquerque's West Mesa. She crunched across the gravel yard to the square concrete porch that fronted the modest house. After double-checking the address against the information on her clipboard, she rang the doorbell.

Twenty seconds of waiting, then the door was opened by a leggy blonde in shorts and a sloppy gray T-shirt. Her feet were bare. Inside the house somewhere, a TV blared cartoon voices.

"Yes?"

"Hi, I'm with the federal Department of Agriculture. I'm looking for Edgar Flanagan. Does he still live at this address?"

It took the blonde a second to process that, then she said, "Oh, you mean Lucky! Nobody calls him Edgar. I couldn't even place the name for a second."

She laughed nervously.

"Did you say Department of *Agriculture*?"

Inez handed over one of her business cards. The woman looked at it for a second.

"Why would you be looking for Lucky?"

"You do know him then?"

"Technically, I'm married to him."

"'Technically?'"

"We've been separated for six months. He doesn't live here anymore."

"Do you know where I can find him?"

The woman looked her over, making Inez glad she'd worn her uniform.

"What could Lucky possibly be into now, that he would draw the attention of an agriculture inspector?"

"I'd be happy to tell you about it, and maybe you could answer some questions for me."

The woman considered that for a moment, then said, "Sure, come on in."

She held the door wide. As Inez went through the doorway, her host said, "I'm Jewel Flanagan."

They awkwardly shook hands. Inez crossed to a blue sofa and sat squarely in the center so Jewel Flanagan wouldn't try to sit next to her. Jewel curled up into an armchair opposite her in a way that made Inez think of her cats.

A little redhaired girl ran into the living room, all smiles and freckles. One look at Inez in her uniform, and she sobered and went straight to her mother. She tried to whisper something to her, but Jewel told her to go finish her TV show while the grown-ups talked. The kid didn't seem to like that answer, but she did as she was told.

"Okay," Jewel said once the child was out of earshot. "What's this about?"

"Food poisoning. It's running rampant, and we think it's due to an illegal shipment of Mexican bologna."

Jewel winced. "I was afraid of that."

"You know about it then?"

"I know Lucky was really sick, throwing up all night."

"When was this?"

"Night before last."

"That fits. That's when the first cases started showing up at emergency rooms."

"God, how sick are they?"

"Nobody has died, that I know of. But some have been sick enough to require hospitalization."

Jewel frowned. "I feel responsible. Lucky only got involved in this business because he was trying to impress me."

"Men do that."

"Yeah, but there's more. I was seeing a man, and he's the one who hired Lucky. I think he's deliberately trying to get Lucky in trouble."

"Given his criminal record, I would say Lucky Flanagan doesn't need help finding trouble."

Jewel nodded. "It finds him. But this time is different. I think he's being set up and he's too dumb to know it."

"I'd like to hear more about this man you were dating. But first, do you know where I can find Lucky?"

"I know where he's staying. I don't know the exact address, but I could take you there."

Inez hesitated. She didn't really want to take the woman with her. On the other hand, it would allow her to keep an eye on Jewel Flanagan, who might otherwise get the itch to warn her husband that Inez was on the way.

"All right."

"Let me call my mother and get her to come look after Scarlett. Just take a second."

Inez took a deep breath. At least the woman wasn't trying to bring the child along with them. That would've been more than Inez could bear.

Chapter 51

By the time they reached the first rest area, Lucky Flanagan had grown tired of the old man's bitching. Señor Villa complained about the arid scenery and Lucky's driving and the condition of American highways and everything else under the sun. The rest area would give Lucky a chance to rest his ears.

"You need a bathroom?" he asked his passenger.

"I'm an old man. I always need a bathroom."

"Right."

"Never pass one up."

"Gotcha."

Lucky turned on his blinker and slowed as they reached the exit ramp. The Mustang's tires growled as he drifted onto the asphalt shoulder, which was grooved to make a warning track.

"Jesus," Señor Villa said, "can't you keep it on the road?"

Lucky didn't reply. He braked the car, slowing to a crawl as they reached the parking area in front of the adobe-style building.

He killed the engine, and they got out of the Mustang. Lucky paused to stretch while Señor Villa hurried to the men's room. Lucky took his time, wandering around, enjoying the quiet, but he didn't stray from the designated walkways. Signs warned of rattlesnakes hiding among the rocks and bushes, and that was bad luck he didn't need.

By the time he meandered over to the restroom, Villa was coming out and they passed at the doorway. Before the old man could start complaining again, Lucky said, "Wait by the car. I'll be right out."

Señor Villa grumbled something, but Lucky didn't catch it and didn't care. He went into the men's room and took his time, washing his face and hands and combing his hair while he was in there.

He clamped his black sunglasses on his face as he stepped outside. The Mustang was right where he'd left it, but there was no sign of Señor Villa. Lucky walked over to the car, trying to see better through the glare on the windshield, but Villa wasn't inside.

Lucky searched the rest area. A dozen vehicles were parked there, some empty, some occupied, but none of the travelers were Señor Villa. Lucky trotted along the sidewalks, checking the picnic tables and the surrounding desert, but turned up nothing.

As panic set in, Lucky was distracted by a couple of familiar faces. An open Jeep had pulled into the parking area, and its occupants now strolled toward him. Lucky recognized the sun-tanned scalps and brawny physiques from forty feet away.

The Badass Brothers.

Lucky's first thought: *How did those two creeps get into the United States? I've been sweating every minute of every border crossing, but these tattooed felons are waved inside? How could any border inspector think they'd be a welcome addition to the citizenry?*

The brothers stopped when they reached him, and stood with their hands on their hips, their white tank tops showing off the thick muscles flexing in their inked-up arms.

"Do you guys practice that?" Lucky said. "Moving right together like that? Have you considered synchronized swimming?"

As he'd figured, the brothers didn't have enough grasp of English to track what he said. They had only one thing on their minds. The taller one said, "José Villa."

Lucky shrugged elaborately. He pointed at the restroom.

"I went in there. When I came back out, he was gone."

Their faces were screwed up, trying to process what he'd said. Lucky threw his hands in the air and said, "Poof!"

Then they got it. Villa was gone. They looked at each other, silently communicating, then turned back to Lucky.

"Where?"

"I don't know where he went. I'm looking for him myself."

They scowled at him. He shrugged some more.

This pantomime was interrupted by a plump older man who wore a blue nylon windbreaker despite the heat. His matching blue baseball cap bore white stitching across the front that said "SNOWBIRD."

"Hey, fellas," he said. "You looking for that older gentleman who rode in with you?"

"Yes!" Lucky beamed at the fat man. "That's my uncle. Did you see where he went?"

"I usually mind my own business, you know, but I did happen to notice when he left. It seemed kinda funny to me that he would arrive in a car and then get in a pickup truck to leave."

"A pickup?"

"Chevy, I think. Silver."

"Headed north?"

"Well, son, you really can't go any other direction out of this rest area—"

"Who was driving?"

"Another old man." He chuckled. "About my own age, I guess. He was wearing a straw cowboy hat."

Lucky turned to the Badass Brothers, and found them studying him intently, as if he were responsible for translating.

"Villa left in a silver truck," Lucky said to them. "I have no idea what he thinks he's doing."

The taller brother spoke in rapid Spanish, apparently translating what Lucky had said. When he was done, the brothers exchanged a loaded look and took a step closer to Lucky.

"It is a race now," the taller one said. "To find him."

"I guess you could say that," Lucky said. "Whoever finds him first will naturally—"

The shorter brother didn't let him finish. He threw a sucker punch into Lucky's midsection. The punch felt like it went all the way through to his backbone. Air rushed out of his lungs, and he collapsed forward, his arms wrapped around his gut as he fell to his knees.

"Hey, now," the snowbird protested. But the Good Samaritan was moving away from the menacing brothers, making good time for a fat man. No help there.

Directly in front of Lucky, the taller Badass Brother squared up, a look of concentration on his face. He did a little soccer-style feint with his shoulders, then kicked Lucky right in the chin.

Lucky's sunglasses went flying as he flipped backward onto the gritty sidewalk. His head cracked against the concrete, and he went dizzy, on the verge of blacking out. He pulled his knees up to his chest, expecting the Badass Brothers to finish him off.

But their footfalls – and harsh laughter – went the other direction. They strode back to their Jeep. By the time Lucky could sit up, the brown Jeep was roaring past, on its way to the interstate, getting a head start.

The snowbird and a scrawny woman with curly gray hair hustled over to Lucky as soon as the brothers were gone.

"Good Lord," the man said. "What was that about?"

"Are you all right?" the woman asked.

Lucky couldn't formulate answers. Instead, he crawled gasping over to his sunglasses and clamped them crookedly onto his face. Then he tried to stand, getting help from the two bystanders.

Once he was on his feet, he had second thoughts about standing. He teetered there, the old couple braced to catch him, until he found his balance. His breath rattled in his lungs as he walked toward the Mustang.

"Son, are you sure you're all right to drive?" the man asked.

"You might have a concussion," the woman added.

Lucky waved them away and got behind the wheel. He managed to fit the key into the ignition and crank the engine to life.

The snowbirds still chirped at him, trying to persuade him to wait, but this was no time for safety considerations. He needed to find Señor Villa. And fast.

Chapter 52

The dusty interior of the silver truck smelled of hay and tobacco smoke and manure.

José Villa's new friend was a farmer named Victor Chavez, who spoke Spanish with the regional accent of rural New Mexico. It sounded oddly old-fashioned to José's ears, but it was no barrier to wide-ranging conversation. They agreed on most of the things they discussed: the need for rain, the foolishness of reckless drivers, the foibles of youth, the wisdom of age.

José told the weathered old man that he'd been riding with his son-in-law – a gringo with red hair – when they'd had a disagreement. That's why José had asked for a ride away from the rest area.

"You're teaching him a lesson," the farmer said.

"Perhaps. He seems like a slow learner."

"But a fast driver? That's not a good combination."

"Lot of it going around," José said.

"Oh, *sí*. A regular epidemic."

The old men laughed together. Victor wheezed and coughed into his hand, then wiped his palm on his faded jeans.

They were poking along at close to the posted speed limit, other vehicles zipping by in the fast lane. As a semi roared past, José spotted a blue sign alongside the highway shoulder: "Rest Area, 2 Miles."

"Ah," he said, pointing. "I should get off there."

"Need to piss again so soon?"

"Don't you?"

More laughter, but Victor said, "It's not that far to my home. You could use my phone to call your son-in-law."

"I can wait for him at the rest area."

"Think he'll find you?"

"He'll figure it out. Eventually."

Victor steered them into the rest area. All the structures were made of dark stained wood with walkways connecting the restrooms to sheltered picnic areas. Very primitive and blocky, but somehow it fit out here in the rolling desert.

The farmer pulled to a stop in a parking spot just past the restrooms. The men shook hands and José started to get out of the truck.

"Hey, Victor," he said. "You know it's dangerous to pick up hitchhikers, right?"

"Oh, I would never offer a ride to any of these young hippies you see along the highway. But you looked as old and broke-down as I am. I figured it was safe."

José smiled. "You guessed right."

He closed the door and went to the sidewalk. He waved as the silver truck pulled away. His new friend waved back, his arm hanging out the window as the pickup rumbled toward the freeway.

Once the truck was out of sight, José turned and squinted into the distance to where the interstate disappeared to the south. He couldn't see a blue Mustang, not yet. But Lucky would be along soon. Probably be hopping mad. The thought made José smile.

He thumped along one of the wooden walkways to a sheltered picnic table. He settled at the table, occupying a slice of shade with a view of the arriving cars. Hot out here, but not too bad in the shade.

He figured he didn't have long to wait.

Chapter 53

Lucky raced north at close to 90 mph, but he was distracted from his driving by the rear-view mirror, where he watched a purpling lump grow on his jaw from the kick to the face. His jawbone ached, but his teeth seemed okay. His stomach muscles, already sore from all-night puking, clenched with pain around the spot where the Badass Brother's fist had deflated him.

The brothers could've decided to do a full soccer practice on his noggin after he was on the ground, defenseless. Instead, they'd hurried away after Señor Villa. What the hell did that *mean*?

The secret recipe. That must be it. Señor Villa had valuable knowledge. That's why Daniel Delgado wanted him in Albuquerque. And that's why Marco Rivera had dispatched the Badass Brothers to bring Villa back.

Lucky, hapless as ever, had stumbled right into a big mess. The two rich young men were in a cross-border pissing match, the future of Rojo on the line.

It occurred to him that the Badass Brothers might not bother to take Señor Villa back to Juarez. They might just leave him dead. That would solve their boss' problem without a lot of fuss at the border. Lucky's heart hammered at the thought.

What had the old man been thinking, riding off with a stranger? And how had he managed it so quickly? Lucky was only in the restroom for five minutes. That was enough time for Villa to strike up a conversation with somebody and catch a ride?

Or, and Lucky got a chill at this thought: Maybe the cowboy in the silver pickup truck *wasn't* a random stranger. Maybe he was somebody sent to pick up Villa. But sent by whom? And why?

Lucky thought about Freddie Garcia and the butcher shop in Albuquerque. Did Villa know that was their destination? Did the Badass Brothers know it, too? He decided he'd warn Garcia, just in case. He wrestled his cell phone out of his pants pocket and punched buttons to get to Garcia's phone number. It rang once.

"Hullo?"

"Hey, Freddie, this is Lucky Flanagan."

"Yes?"

"Um, we've got a little problem. Can we talk about it on this phone?"

A pause, then Garcia said, "Go ahead."

Lucky told him about Villa's disappearance at the rest area, the beatdown in the parking lot and the current race against the Badass Brothers, who were after the old man.

"Who did Villa ride away with?"

"I don't know," Lucky said. "Some guy in a cowboy hat. I thought you might have a guess."

"Beats me."

"Whoever he is, he's got the Badass Brothers right on his heels," Lucky said.

"You're chasing after them?"

"They got a head start while I was rolling around on the sidewalk, but I might catch them. I'm driving as fast as I dare."

"It's real important that we get Villa back," Garcia said. "But don't risk your life doing it. Sounds like these brothers are dangerous."

"You'll find out how dangerous if they show up at the butcher shop."

"You're kidding, right? I've got half a dozen butchers out there, using knives and cleavers on meat. You think they'd let a couple of punks come in here after me?"

"I just wanted to warn you."

"Consider me warned. Now get off the phone and concentrate on finding Señor Villa."

Lucky pocketed the phone. He put both hands on the wheel and pressed the accelerator, nudging the speedometer upward a few clicks. If he got pulled over by a cop, the race would be over. But he had to take his chances if he hoped to catch up.

Chapter 54

Ralph Rolfe had been home from work only a few minutes when his doorbell rang. He jumped at the unfamiliar noise. He almost never had visitors. When he did, they were friends like Lucky, who didn't bother with the doorbell.

Ralph shuffled though the living room, frowning at the snack bags and empty bottles that littered the coffee table. He pulled the interior door closed behind him as he went onto the screened-in porch.

He was surprised to find two women on the front stoop. The tall blonde he recognized as Jewel, the almost-ex-wife of Lucky Flanagan. The other was stout and stern and dressed in some sort of uniform with a badge on her white shirt.

Ralph gulped at the sight of that gold badge – he'd never had good experiences with authority figures – but he opened the creaky screen door and squeaked, "Yes?"

"Is Lucky home yet?" Jewel asked.

"No. I haven't heard from him."

He started to turn away.

"Do you know where he went today?" the uniformed woman asked. "What he's doing?"

He shook his head, but he knew they could see right through him. Ralph had always been the most transparent liar, fumbling his words, his cheeks flushed. Most of the time, he simply told the truth. It was the only way to avoid the anxiety of defending a shaky lie.

"Come on, Ralph," Jewel said. "This is important."

Ralph sighed. He knew he couldn't stand up to an interrogation. Might as well get it finished.

"He went to Juarez."

"I knew that much," Jewel said. "He called me when he was driving down there."

"Then why—"

"Shouldn't he be back by now?"

"I don't know," Ralph said. "Depends on how long he was stuck in traffic at the border—"

"Tell her," Jewel said. "Tell her what he's transporting today."

Ralph hung his head, but it did nothing to prevent the words from spilling from his mouth.

"He was driving a person this time. Señor José Villa. Do you know who that is?"

The women shook their heads.

"He's, like, the inventor of Rojo bologna," he said. "He knows the secret recipe."

"Why is he coming up here?" Jewel asked.

"Retirement," Ralph said. "But he's gonna cash out first."

"By selling that recipe?"

He nodded. "Makes sense, doesn't it?"

"His partners must not like that very much," Jewel said.

"I said the same thing! I told Lucky, if I were those guys, I wouldn't let Villa leave Mexico alive."

The women exchanged a look. The uniformed one said, "Do you know where Lucky was taking this man?"

"I think he was going to a butcher shop in the South Valley. The one where Lucky delivered the bologna."

She took a step toward him, as if barely controlling herself from pouncing on him. But her voice was strangely calm as she said, "Do you know the name of this butcher shop?"

"No, I don't." Ralph turned to Jewel. "But you could probably figure it out. It's the one that's owned by your boyfriend."

Jewel's face flushed, but she managed a weak smile.

"He's not my 'boyfriend' anymore," she said. "But I know which butcher shop you mean."

She turned to the other woman. "Should we go there next?"

"Might be dangerous. Are you sure you're up for that?"

Ralph's pulse quickened at the thought of the two women facing danger at the butcher shop. Before he knew what he was doing, he blurted, "I'll go with you!"

Chapter 55

The Barreras brothers drove for half an hour in silence before Tino finally shouted over the wind, "I must admit, I was surprised when Villa's driver turned out to be that redhead."

His brother nodded, and said, "Not as surprised as the redhead when I hit him in the gut."

Tino smiled, remembering the look of astonishment on the gringo's face. Just like an American, thinking he could talk his way out of every problem. Sometimes, it's too late for talk.

"And that kick of yours," Tito said. "A thing of beauty."

"Gracias. Still, the gringo is behind us somewhere. Would've been better to leave him dead."

"Too many witnesses."

"I know. That many, it's a problem."

They drove along in silence for a few minutes. Tino felt sure his brother was busy with the same mental calculations as him: How many witnesses would've needed to be killed? How many is too many?

"The boss wants this done quietly," Tino said finally.

Tito nodded.

After another minute's lumbering thought, Tino said, "I wonder if Villa somehow learned we were behind them. Maybe that's why he switched cars."

"Maybe," Tito said, "Villa realized he was being driven north by a redheaded idiot."

Tino considered that. It sounded plausible. Señor Villa didn't suffer fools, gladly or otherwise. More than once, the old man had spoken sharply to the brothers. He thought he could get away with it because he was elderly.

"I want to kill the old man," Tino said.

His brother nodded vigorously.

"And I want to take my time doing it."

"We can start by cutting out his tongue," Tito offered. "So

we don't have to listen to him while we work."

"Good idea."

A blue sign flashed past, and Tino barely translated the English before it was gone from sight.

"A rest area," he told his brother. "Two miles ahead."

"I don't need it," Tito said.

"Not for you. For Villa. Old men always need to stop at bathrooms."

"We should check it out. Maybe the silver truck will be there."

Tino turned on his blinker.

Chapter 56

Lucky Flanagan couldn't decide at first whether to exit at the rest area. He moved into the slow lane and let off the gas, thinking. Would Señor Villa get off the freeway for a pee break while in the midst of fleeing? It seemed unlikely, but Villa's aged bladder might demand a stop. It was worth checking out, and it wouldn't take long—

A trucker behind him laid down on his air horn, startling Lucky into a decision. He swerved into the turn lane for the rest area and turned on his blinker to signal that's what he'd meant all along. The semi blew past in a huff.

The buildings and picnic pavilions in the rest area were made of dark wood, so the whole thing appeared to be assembled of Lincoln Logs, plunked down on a parched hillside. The few trees standing around looked limp from the heat.

He let the Mustang creep through the parking lot toward the restrooms, but he saw no sign of Señor Villa or a silver truck. Instead, he found a brown Jeep parked at the curb.

The Badass Brothers came out of the men's room at that moment. They were looking around, the sunlight gleaming on their shaved heads. Were they looking for Señor Villa? Or had they left him in that bathroom? Lucky felt anger well up, a hot bubble inside his chest. These two hadn't hesitated when it came to roughing up Lucky. Had they done the same to the old man? Worse?

The brothers spotted him in the creeping Mustang. They boldly walked out into the middle of the narrow parking lot, blocking his path, their hands raised in the international signal for "halt."

Lucky had a different idea.

He goosed the accelerator and the Mustang leaped forward. The brothers went wide-eyed at the sudden surge. They tried to run out of the way, but in their confusion, they smacked into each other, nose to nose, squarely in front of the Mustang's hood.

The taller one realized his mistake and tried to spin away, but Lucky gave the steering wheel a little yank to the left, so he could catch both brothers with the front of the car. The shorter brother bounced up onto the hood and splatted against the windshield like a bug. The taller one, clipped by the left fender, went tumbling across the asphalt.

Lucky hit the brakes, and his windshield cleared as the shorter brother slid off the hood into the parking lot. He threw the gearshift into reverse and backed up far enough that he could see both brothers writhing in pain on the pavement. He resisted the temptation to run over them, instead picking a clear path between the two.

Lucky spotted Señor Villa as the old man walked out of a picnic pavilion, waving his scrawny arms over his head.

He had to control himself to keep from running over Villa, too. Once you start mowing people down with your car, it's hard to stop. Other people in the rest area seemed to sense this as they ran for cover.

He stopped at the curb right in front of Señor Villa, who opened the door and ducked into the passenger seat, cool as you please.

Lucky checked his rear-view. One of the Badass Brothers was on feet, though he seemed to be limping in circles. The other one was on all fours, blood dripping from his forehead.

Grinning, Lucky looked over at Señor Villa. They both wore sunglasses, so it was hard to tell for sure, but the old man didn't look particularly happy to see him.

"The fuck are you waiting for?" he grumbled. "Let's get out of here."

Chapter 57

José Villa buckled his seat belt as the Mustang lurched onto the highway, gaining speed.

"What the hell, man?" Lucky shouted over the roar of the engine. "Where did you go?"

"I took a ride with a farmer," José said. "An interesting man who, I must say, is a much safer driver than you are."

"Why did you *do* that? You scared the shit out of me."

"A little joke," José said. "Repayment for that long, hot walk across the bridge to El Paso."

"You nearly gave me a heart attack!"

"Oh, you're all right."

"Look at my jaw! See that bruise? I got that from those brothers while I was looking for you."

José looked over his shoulder, half-expecting to see the Jeep driven by the Badass Brothers gaining on them. But it wasn't back there. Not yet.

Only then did he let the laughter come bubbling forth. He laughed so hard, he was slapping his bony knees.

Lucky, teeth clenched behind the wheel, apparently didn't see the humor in the situation.

"Those two assholes," the old man wheezed, "the way they went flying into the air when you hit them with your car. Best thing I've ever seen."

He collapsed into laughter again, remembering the Badass Brothers brought low, bleeding in a rest area parking lot. He wished he'd taken a photograph to send to Marco.

"I'm glad you find this so entertaining," Lucky said. "We could've been killed back there."

"Not a scratch on me!" José countered. "More than those brothers can say for themselves."

"They weren't hurt very bad," Lucky said. "They'll chase after us soon as one of them can see well enough to drive."

José cackled.

"That moment when you ran into them," he said, "it was like slow motion. They crashed into each other, then *you* crashed into them both. If they hadn't been so stupid, they could've gotten out of the way."

"The Two Stooges."

"Marco can be the third one," José said. "The bossy one. What was his name? Moe. That's Marco. His father, Roberto, was a gentleman, a pleasure to know. Now, I've got Moe."

"Why did he send those guys after you?"

José hesitated. He wasn't sure how much the gringo knew.

"Is it the secret recipe?" Lucky said. "Is that what this is about?"

"Marco is crazy when it comes to protecting the Rojo recipe," José said. "He's afraid I will sell the recipe to your employer."

Lucky winced at the word "employer," but he said, "Is that your plan? To sell the recipe to Daniel Delgado?"

"Yes."

"For a lot of money."

"You bet your ass."

"But first," Lucky said, "I have to get *both* of our asses to Albuquerque before those brothers catch us."

"Correct."

"And if they catch up to us first?"

"They'll probably kill me," José said. "It's the one way to make sure I never tell anyone the recipe."

"And if I'm with you, they'll kill me, too," Lucky said.

They chewed on that for a minute, then Lucky said, "You're telling me that we literally could *die* today. Over *bologna*."

"People die for less all the time. In Mexico, people die for much less."

"This isn't Mexico."

José looked out the window at the thunderclouds massing over the rolling hills. The distant farmhouses were flat-roofed adobes, rundown and dusty. The scattered cattle looked hungry.

"It's close enough," he said.

Chapter 58

When the phone rang in Freddie Garcia's office, he expected it to be Lucky Flanagan again, with something else gone wrong. Freddie's heart tripped when he saw the readout said, "Daniel Delgado."

"*Hola*," Freddie said. "I've been trying to reach you for hours."

"I was in meetings. What's up?"

"A lot. That USDA inspector came back. More questions about Rojo. The Hernandez brothers told her they got it from us."

"Those assholes."

"She closed them down," Freddie said. "And she was gonna do the same to us."

"What did you do?"

"I told her there *was* a smuggler who was responsible for the Rojo moving into town, but it wasn't anyone connected to us."

"Did you give her a name?"

"I told her it was Lucky Flanagan."

Delgado laughed, a sharp bark.

"I like it," he said, "but won't he sic her right back on us?"

"His word against ours. Who's going to believe that loser?"

Delgado thought it over for a second, then said, "So if anybody has to take a fall for any of this, it'll be Lucky."

"I figured that was what you'd want," Freddie said coldly, "given your relationship with his wife."

Nothing for a second, then Daniel Delgado laughed again.

"You think that's what this is about? That's hilarious."

"Why is that?"

"Because she broke up with me. We won't be seeing each other anymore. I dragged Lucky Flanagan into our operation for nothing."

"He's worked out all right so far," Freddie said. "But he's got his hands full today."

"What's going on?" A little too much glee in Delgado's

voice. Still enjoying Lucky's troubles.

"He lost José Villa."

"*What*?"

"Long story. I just got off the phone with Lucky. He found Villa, and they're on their way. They'll be in Albuquerque in an hour or so."

"Good. I'll come to the shop and we can meet there."

"Wait, there's more," Freddie said. "Lucky says your pal Marco Rivera sent a couple of goons after Villa."

"This side of the border?"

"They crossed paths with our guys at a rest area, and Lucky and Villa barely got away. Lucky thinks Marco's people might be headed here to the shop. Maybe you want to meet with Villa somewhere else."

A pause.

"No, this will work," Delgado said. "Close the shop a little early. Send your people home."

"Don't you think we might need them?"

"As what, witnesses? We can manage things on our own, Federico."

"But if those two show up here—"

"If they do, we'll take care of it."

"That could get messy."

"It's a butcher shop," Delgado said. "We can always hose the place down."

Freddie didn't like the sound of that. He looked out at his pristine shop. One of his butchers, Jorge, had a pork loin laid out on a cutting board, and was using a cleaver to hack it into precise inch-thick chops.

"Once I've got Villa," Delgado said, "I'll keep him under wraps until we're sure Marco's boys have gone back to Mexico empty-handed."

"What about the inspector? I don't want her closing the shop. I owe it to my employees—"

"She'll go after Lucky now. And he's slippery enough to keep her busy for days."

"But what about those cases of food poisoning? We could be looking at lawsuits."

"You worry too much."

"Maybe you don't worry enough."

"It's just business, Freddie. I'll see you in an hour."

Chapter 59

Jewel Flanagan watched from the passenger seat of Inez Montoya's government Ford as storm clouds roiled the sky. A bank of dark clouds pushed northward from the southwest, obliterating the sunset.

As she leaned forward to see the clouds directly above them, a fat raindrop splatted against the windshield, so loud it startled her. Three more huge drops quickly cluttered the windshield. Raindrops clattered on the roof of the car.

"Great," Inez said. "*Now* the monsoon arrives."

"We need the rain," Ralph Rolfe said from the back seat. The automatic response of desert dwellers everywhere.

"It's bad timing," Inez said. "We can't see if it's raining."

They were parked in the lot of a boarded-up hair salon that sat directly across busy Isleta Boulevard from *El Matador Carnicería*, and rain ruined the view.

"Turn on the wipers again," Jewel said.

Inez did it, but she said, "We can't just sit here with the wipers going. Somebody will notice."

The only one still in the shop appeared to be the manager, a slick-haired man Inez had identified as Freddie Garcia. He was mostly out of sight, but once in a while they'd spot him through the front windows, pacing and looking at his wristwatch.

"There he is again," Ralph said as Garcia came to the front door of the shop. He looked up and down Isleta and up at the storm, then shook his head and went back into the shadows.

"You think he's waiting for Lucky?" Jewel asked.

"Probably," Ralph said. "You want me to call Lucky and see if he's getting close?"

"Good God, no," Inez said. "If you alert him that we're watching, he might take off and take Villa with him. I need to talk to that old man."

"Right, sorry," Ralph said. "I'm just worried. What if we're letting Lucky walk into some sort of ambush?"

"You read too many comic books," Jewel said.

"You have no idea. But that doesn't mean I'm wrong."

Jewel had no answer for that. More rain peppered the car, and the clouds looked ready to let loose. Passing cars were using their headlights, which further obscured the view of *El Matador*.

"Maybe we need to move closer," Jewel said.

"They'll spot us," Inez said. "We can't risk that. Not until Villa gets here."

Ralph started to chime in, saying, "What about the—"

He stopped, his breath catching, as a car steered into the parking lot of the butcher shop.

Inez risked the wipers again.

"Is that Lucky's car?

The car was sleek and low, its silvery skin reflecting the streetlights. Jewel recognized it right away.

"Not hardly," she said. "That's a Jaguar."

"Oh, yeah," Ralph said. "In his *dreams*, Lucky has that car."

"That's Daniel Delgado's car."

Jewel felt heat rise within her at the sight of the Jag. It was one of the lures Daniel dangled in front of women like her. Now that she knew what a user he was, it made Jewel angry that she'd fallen for his wiles and his wealth.

The Jaguar disappeared behind the butcher shop. They watched as raindrops covered the windshield, but the silver car didn't reappear.

"He must've gone inside," Inez said. "If Lucky and Villa do show up, we'll have all the players in one place."

"Then what happens?" Jewel asked.

It took Inez a long time to answer. Too long.

"I'll do my duty," she said finally.

Her voice had steel in it, but that didn't make Jewel feel any better.

"Couldn't it be dangerous?" she asked. "Shouldn't we call the police?"

"And tell them what?" Inez said. "That someone is selling a bologna recipe?"

Ralph snorted, and Jewel could feel herself blushing. She said, "Lucky could get caught in the middle of whatever they're doing here."

"It'll be all right," Ralph said. "It's only bologna. What's the worst that could happen?"

Jewel sighed. She was afraid to think about the worst.

Chapter 60

José Villa felt like he'd escaped death as the blue Mustang splashed into the parking lot of the butcher shop. His idiot driver, the redhead who answered to "Lucky," as if he were a *dog*, drove even worse once they arrived in stormy Albuquerque. They'd zoomed through ever-thickening traffic on the freeway and finally got off onto wet surface streets to reach this place, surprisingly intact.

The car fishtailed across a wide puddle in the parking lot, and José couldn't take it anymore.

"Slow down, stupid. Don't kill us at the last minute."

"I want to get inside."

"What's the hurry?"

"I don't like storms. The lightning and all."

"You're afraid of lightning?"

"It's a long story. Let's just get indoors before it gets worse."

Lucky steered the Mustang around to the rear of the building. Only a few vehicles back here, including a very nice silver Jaguar and a big white truck that José recognized as the one they'd used to smuggle the Rojo. He idly wondered what they would use the truck for now.

Lights burned brightly in an office that occupied the back corner of the building. Rain ran down the windows, but he could make out the shapes of two men inside, sitting across from each other at a desk. One was brawny and wore a dark shirt with long sleeves. The other was slight and seemed to be wearing a black suit. He had a relaxed posture, leaning back in the chair with his legs crossed, and José decided he must be the wealthy Daniel Delgado.

Lucky pulled the Mustang up to the back of the building, so his headlights shone into the office windows. He cut off the lights and the engine.

"Hang on," he said to José. "Give them time to get the door unlocked. We're going to get drenched."

"Don't you have an umbrella?"

"This is New Mexico, man. You don't need an umbrella. If it's raining, you just wait until it's done."

"We don't want to wait now?"

"I'd like to get inside."

José could see through the rain-glazed windows that the men inside were rising to go to the back door.

Naturally, the pace of the rainfall picked up at that moment. With the wipers now shut off, they quickly couldn't see out the windshield. Rain thundered on the roof of the car.

"Great," Lucky said. "Okay, look over there. Soon as that back door opens, jump out and run for it. I'll be right behind you."

Lucky put his hand on the door handle, ready to go, then paused. "What about your luggage?"

"I don't want my stuff to get soaked," José said. "We can bring it in after the rain stops."

He had his eyes on the back door, squinting against the blur of the rain. He couldn't be sure, but he thought the door opened a crack.

"There you go," Lucky confirmed. "Go. Quick as you can."

José threw open the door and clambered out into the icy rain. His clothes were instantly soaked, and he wished he'd waited in the car. He hurried to the back door, his loafers slipping on the steaming asphalt.

He could hear Lucky's shoes slapping the pavement as the redhead ran around the back end of the Mustang and followed him to the door. They skated inside, sliding on the wet concrete floor, and José found himself caught in the arms of the brawnier of the two men he'd seen through the windows.

The man was dressed like a cowboy – boots and tight jeans and a brown Western-style shirt – but his slicked-back hair looked too perfect to be ruined by a hat. Soon as he realized how sopping José was, he let go of him and took a step back. The other man, slender in his elegant suit, stood out of harm's way, an amused smile on his face as he looked over the dripping travelers.

Thunder boomed and the brawny man stepped around José to slam the steel door and block out the rain.

"Wow, what a storm," Lucky said. "The monsoons finally arrive, just as we're trying to get indoors."

"That's the way it always goes," the big man said.

He introduced himself as Freddie Garcia and asked if José would like a towel. José nodded, and Garcia went into the butcher shop's work area in search of clean towels.

"You probably gathered by now that I'm Daniel Delgado," said the man in the suit. He didn't offer to shake José's hand. In fact, his hands were in the pockets of his suit coat, as if he were afraid they'd get wet. José thinking: *He's probably worried about his fucking manicure.*

"What happened to your face?" Delgado said to Lucky. The purple lump on the gringo's jaw continued to grow. It looked like he was holding a plum in his cheek.

"Shaving accident," Lucky said.

Delgado smirked, but he didn't pursue it.

Garcia returned with three white hand towels. He gave one to José and one to Lucky. The third he tossed onto the puddle that had pooled just inside the back door. The towels were barely big enough to dry their faces and arms, but they were better than nothing.

Once they'd dried off, Delgado said casually, "Freddie, mind if Señor Villa and I use your office for a minute?"

"Sure. Go ahead."

"Wait out here with Lucky until we're done. Shouldn't be long. Then you can lock the place up."

"Will do."

Delgado held the door so José could go inside. The air-conditioner was running in the office, and he was instantly chilled. José perched on a wooden chair that wouldn't be harmed by his wet clothes, and Delgado sat in the swivel chair behind the desk. He crossed his legs and smiled at José.

"Welcome to the United States of America," Delgado said.

"We're happy to have you here."

José thanked him, but he wanted to keep the pleasantries brief. He was shivering.

"I hear Marco Rivera is quite upset that you left Mexico."

José arched an eyebrow at him. "You know Marco?"

"Oh, sure. We went to college together, right here in Albuquerque. Didn't you know Marco was briefly educated up here?"

José frowned. He hadn't understood the connection until now.

"I didn't know he was educated at all," he muttered. "I've always thought he was a punk."

Delgado smiled.

"I can't disagree with that," he said. "He got into lots of trouble at UNM. I think they kicked him out after a year."

"That sounds like Marco."

They studied each other for a moment. Lucky and Freddie Garcia stood outside the glass door, whispering, trying to act like they weren't watching every move inside the office.

"Freddie tells me that Marco sent a couple of tough guys after you," Delgado said. "They're right on your heels?"

"They're idiots. We don't have to worry about them."

"You sure?"

"Lucky ran over them with his car."

"*What*?"

"He was going slow, but they still got hurt. They won't be bothering anybody for a while."

"When Lucky told us about those guys chasing after you, it got me to thinking: What if something happened to you? You know, God forbid, you had a heart attack or something? Then what? We would've gone to all this trouble for nothing."

"Because if I die, the recipe dies with me."

"I was thinking, maybe you could write it down for me. We could lock it up here in Freddie's office, or at a place of your choosing. But there would be a written record. Just in case."

José narrowed his eyes at the younger man.

"You need to pay me first. Then I'll write it down."

Delgado nodded, as if that was what he'd expected. He slipped his hand into the pocket of his jacket and came out with a stubby black pistol.

"I'm afraid I must insist, Señor Villa," he said. "It's just a precaution, you understand. But it's a precaution we need to take."

It took an effort, but José tore his gaze away from the black gun. He looked Delgado in the eye.

"So, you're a punk, too?"

Delgado picked up a pen and a legal pad and tossed them across the cluttered desk to José.

"Write it down."

"You won't shoot me," José said. "If I'm dead, you've got nothing. As long as the recipe stays in my head, you've got to keep me alive."

"I could shoot you in the leg. I could shoot you in the foot. You wouldn't die and, sooner or later, you'd write it down. Let's skip the hard part. You'll get your money soon, I promise, but I'll have my insurance in the meantime. Write down the recipe. Then I'll take you out for a nice dinner at my favorite restaurant. How does that sound?"

José said nothing.

"Better than a bullet in the leg, right?"

Thunder rolled overhead, rattling the windows.

Chapter 61

Lucky was stunned when he saw the black pistol in Daniel Delgado's fist. What the hell was going on in that office?

He reached for the doorknob, but a heavy hand slapped onto his shoulder.

"Hold on," Freddie Garcia said. "Let this play out."

"He's got a gun."

"He's not gonna shoot anybody. He's a businessman."

Lucky shrugged off Garcia's hand and threw open the office door. As he stepped through the doorway, Delgado shifted the pistol's aim slightly, so it pointed directly at Lucky's chest. Lucky's feet did a little dance, as if reminding him they knew how to run, but he held his ground.

"Hey, c'mon," he said. "Put that gun away. No reason for anybody to get hurt here."

"You interrupted our conversation," Delgado said. "That's rude."

"I'm often rude. It's how I've gotten so far in life."

Delgado snorted and the other two laughed, a little too heartily for Lucky's tastes, but he let it go. Laughter's better than slaughter.

Thunder roared overhead, and Lucky jumped. *Goddamn, why does there have to be a lightning storm now?* His nerves were strung tight.

Delgado held up a finger, waiting for a chance to speak. When the thunder stopped rumbling, he said, "Señor Villa was about to write down the Rojo recipe for me."

"He was?"

"A written record," Delgado said. "For safekeeping."

Lucky turned to the old man, who sat shivering on the wooden chair.

"Is that right? Were you giving him the recipe?"

Señor Villa's mouth was set in a thin line. He shook his head.

"He doesn't think I'll really shoot him," Delgado said. "Maybe I'll shoot you instead."

"Why would you do that?"

"To prove a point. Señor Villa might take a different position once he sees I'm serious."

"We can tell you're serious," Lucky said. "The gun says that for you. But shooting us would make a lot of noise. Big mess in Freddie's office. Put the gun away."

Behind him, Freddie Garcia had filled the doorway. He, too, pleaded with Delgado.

"Come on, boss. Let's talk like businessmen."

"It's getting crowded in here," Delgado said as he got to his feet. The gun's aim never wavered from Lucky's chest. "Let's go out into the shop where there's more room."

Garcia backed out of the way so Lucky could come through the door. Lucky turned and held the door open for Señor Villa, who creaked to his feet and followed. Once they were out of the office, Delgado gestured them toward the center of the workspace with his gun.

"Over there," he said. "Where there's a drain in the floor."

Lucky didn't like the sound of that, but he did as he was told. He and Señor Villa stood damply side by side. Delgado stood directly in front of them, the pistol casually pointed their way. Freddie Garcia was off to Lucky's left, out of the way, standing next to a butcher table that held a rack full of knives and cleavers.

Rain lashed at the windows, obscuring the headlights of vehicles roaring past on Isleta Boulevard. Lucky wished he were out there right now, squinting in traffic rather than staring down a gun. Since he had no choice in the matter, he decided to speak up.

"This is about Jewel, isn't it? You want me out of the way, so you can have her to yourself."

"God, you're a moron," Delgado said. "I'm not even seeing her anymore. This was never about love. It's about money."

"Then why do you need the gun? Pay the man and we're

good."

"It's also about keeping secrets. I don't need you anymore, Lucky, and you seem to have a big mouth."

"Fuck you."

The words were out of his mouth before he could stop them. Proving Delgado's point.

Delgado started to answer, but he didn't get the chance. The back door of the butcher shop flung open, banging against the concrete wall as rain pelted inside.

Chapter 62

Inez Montoya didn't see the gun until she was inside the shop, Jewel and Ralph crowding into the doorway behind her, trying to get out of the cold rain. By then, it was too late to change her mind. The door slammed shut behind them.

Daniel Delgado and the rest of them wheeled toward her, but Delgado was the only one with a pistol. Inez wished (and not for the first time) that her job required her to pack a gun. Instead, here she stood, sopping wet, with nothing for protection except a clipboard and a badge.

"Stop right there!" she commanded, a reflex as much as anything. "Put down that gun!"

Delgado didn't put down the gun. He pointed it at her.

"I mean it," she said. "I represent the United States government, and as such, I am the sole authority—"

The little pistol jumped in Delgado's hand. Its report was no louder than a handclap, certainly not as loud as the slamming door, but it still made everyone jump.

Inez looked over her shoulder and saw the perfectly round hole the bullet left in the window nearest the back door. It had missed her by inches.

"Enough," Delgado said pleasantly. "We were in the middle of something, and you interrupted us. Did you bring these people here, Jewel?"

He looked Jewel Flanagan over, as if she were property and he was deciding whether to buy her. Jewel didn't look her best. Her damp T-shirt clung to her shoulders, and her blond hair was wet and falling over her face. She jerked when he said her name.

Inez took a step toward Delgado, ready to intercede, and he pointed the pistol at her.

"Stay back."

"I can't believe you're such an asshole, Daniel," Jewel said, "You'll do anything to get what you want."

"Ah," he said. "Finally, you understand me."

"I understand plenty," she said. "That's why I'm here. To keep you from hurting people with your greedy little hands."

He smiled at her.

"You can't risk shooting anyone," she said. "Your reputation would be ruined."

"I don't care about that."

"You will care," Lucky said, "when your picture's on the front page of the newspaper."

"I'm not worried about bad publicity. I'm looking to the future. I'm going to make a fortune off Señor Villa's secret recipe. You think I'd let any of you stand in my way?"

Behind him, Freddie Garcia said, "Come on, boss. Let's start over on this deal. Señor Villa is here. These other people can fuck off, and we can get on with our business. No harm done. If Señor Villa wants to wait until he's been paid to give you the secret recipe—"

"I want it now," Delgado said.

Inez took another step toward him, though her knees shook. She realized Ralph was hiding behind her, and that didn't make her feel any better. She hadn't expected any help from him or Jewel, other than the safety of numbers, but now she wished she hadn't involved them at all. They were in danger and she was to blame.

Thunder crashed, making everyone start, and Inez worried about Delgado's finger on the trigger. She needed to take control of this situation before someone got killed.

But how?

Chapter 63

"This is bullshit," José Villa growled. "We had a deal, and now you're waving a gun around, threatening innocent people."

Daniel Delgado turned toward him, the pistol training on his chest. It made José's aged heart do a little flamenco, and he felt short of breath. He tried not to let it show.

"We still have a deal," Delgado said. "I was only trying to adjust the timetable. I'll be investing a lot in product development. I deserve to get some insurance before I shell out more money."

"And if I write down the recipe?" José snarled. "Won't you shoot me anyway?"

Delgado arched an eyebrow, like he was considering the option. José wondered if he'd gone too far.

The skinny blonde who'd come in out of the rain suddenly decided to speak again.

"Daniel, please, if I ever meant anything to you, do this for me now. Put the gun down and let us all walk out of here."

Delgado turned toward her. The brawny butcher stood behind him, leaning against a steel work table, but the rest were spread around him like a fan – the uniformed woman and the quivering fat boy who hid behind her to Delgado's left, then the blonde, then Lucky and José. All of them just far enough away that they couldn't make a grab for the pistol.

When the gun pointed at the blonde, Lucky took a step to the side, putting himself between her and Delgado. His bruised face flushed, as if in shock or anger, and José wondered if he'd surprised himself. Maybe his feet had moved by themselves.

"Look at them," José said to Delgado. "Hiding behind each other like scared children. Why do you treat people this way?"

"This is your fault, not mine," Delgado said. "If you'd given me what I asked for, we would've been out to a nice dinner by now, instead of cooped up here in a butcher shop with a bunch of people who smell like wet dogs."

José smiled. At least he was keeping Delgado talking. As long as he was talking, he wasn't shooting.

Chapter 64

Lucky Flanagan's heart knocked in his chest like it was searching for an exit. He wished the old man would stop taunting Daniel Delgado. The little pistol still held enough bullets to put a hole in each one of them; Lucky had done the math. He did not want a bullet hole anywhere in his body. Of that he was certain.

Yet he'd stepped in front of Jewel to shield her when Delgado pointed the gun her way. Was that true love at work? Blind courage? Bad luck? He had a feeling he was about to find out.

José Villa smiled at Delgado, that smug smile he bestowed on idiots, and Lucky winced at whatever he was about to say.

"I don't do business with assholes," Villa said. "And you, sir, have proved to be an asshole."

The gun was pointing at Señor Villa now, and Lucky wondered whether he should make a grab for Delgado's arm. He was taller than Delgado, probably stronger. Maybe he could wrest the gun away. Or, he could get them all killed. Somehow, that seemed a more likely possibility.

Delgado seemed to sense that Lucky was sizing him up. He took a step backward, toward Freddie Garcia, who scowled at all of them, as if they were a complicated puzzle he was trying to solve.

The black hole at the end of little pistol's barrel drifted away from Señor Villa and toward Lucky, who was very conscious of Jewel hiding behind him. If Delgado pulled the trigger, would the bullet go through them both?

"Come on, Daniel," Jewel snapped. "Enough is enough."

Lucky wished very much that she would shut up, but there was no way to convey that message without taking his eyes off Delgado. Instead, he said, "You're outvoted, man. Put the gun away, and we can act like none of this ever happened."

Delgado's expression didn't change, but Lucky saw something harden in his eyes. Not a good sign.

Lightning flashed all around them, filling the windows with white light, followed almost immediately by the crack of thunder.

All the lights winked out, casting the interior into such a sudden darkness that Lucky thought for a second that he'd passed out.

"Fuck." Freddie Garcia's deep voice. "Power's out."

Nothing for a second. Then the sound of the pistol going off, a sharp clap compared to the rumbling thunder.

Lucky whirled, grabbed at Jewel's damp shirt and dragged her to the floor.

Chapter 65

Freddie Garcia stood frozen in the darkness, afraid to move. The acrid gunsmoke made him want to sneeze, but he stifled the urge. Better to not make the slightest noise while the boss was looking for targets in the dark.

The lights flickered back to life, making him blink and squint. Freddie saw that Lucky and his blond wife were on the floor, cowering from the gun. The bearded guy still crouched behind Inez Montoya, like he was trying to crawl right up her ass. Inez stood stock still, eyes wide, her clipboard held before her like a shield. José Villa had his hands in his pants pockets, shoulders thrown back, daring anyone to harm him.

In the midst of them stood Daniel Delgado, his arm extended straight up, the gun still smoking in his hand. White plaster dust drifted down from the ceiling, falling like snow.

"The next bullet," he said, "goes in somebody's head."

A moment of silence, then José Villa said, "You're all talk, just like Marco. Couple of punks."

Delgado pointed the pistol at Señor Villa, who smirked at him. Freddie couldn't take it anymore.

"Come on, boss. Don't shoot him, not here in the shop. The police will come. The government will close the shop. I'll be out of work."

Freddie tried to laugh, maybe lighten the mood, but it came out a bullfrog croak. He coughed into his fist.

Delgado still stood with his back to Freddie, not taking his eyes off the others for a second.

"Not now, Freddie," he said. "I'm deciding which one of these shitbirds to shoot first."

Freddie hadn't signed up for this sort of scene, but he didn't see any way out now. The gun made Delgado crazy with power.

Lightning flashed again, and thunder roared. The lights flickered, but the power stayed on this time.

Then another boom, off to Freddie's left. The back door

banged open, and two figures stepped in from the pouring rain. The men had shaved heads and black tattoos and their wet shirts clung to their pumped-up bodies. They looked almost identical, except one was two inches taller than the other. The shorter one had a huge red scrape across his forehead.

"What the hell?" Delgado said, but Freddie recognized immediately who these guys must be. Marco's boys. The Badass brothers. And they weren't here to talk.

"Wait," Freddie said, but he was too late.

The shorter brother threw something at them, putting so much effort into it he lunged forward onto one knee. The object flashed before Freddie's eyes, too fast to follow, but then it abruptly stopped, and he realized what he was seeing.

A knife. A shiny knife. Now buried to the hilt between the ribs of José Villa, right over his heart. The old man reeled backward, his eyes wide, scarlet blood blossoming on his white shirt.

Jewel screamed.

Delgado's pistol cracked again and again.

At the back door, bright blood spurted from the shorter brother's shoulder and neck. A third bullet struck him in the face, a red dot appearing just below his left eye, and he fell backward, his legs folded under him.

The taller brother had a knife, too, but the barrage of bullets chased him out into the rain. Freddie couldn't tell whether the fucker had been hit, but he limped off into the darkness, which was good enough for now.

Freddie wheeled, just in time to see Señor Villa crumple to the floor.

Chapter 66

While everyone else gaped at the newly dead, Inez Montoya saw her chance. Daniel Delgado's arm was extended toward the back door, where the bloodied skinhead lay in a pile on the concrete floor. Inez swung her wooden clipboard downward like an ax, and the edge cracked against Delgado's wrist bone. The black pistol flew from his hand and skittered across the floor under the butcher tables.

"Goddamnit!" Delgado shouted as he clutched his injured wrist to his chest. "You'll pay for that!"

Lucky Flanagan, still on the floor with Jewel, took off after the gun, scrambling on all fours through the maze of steel table legs. Ralph, too, started to move toward the pistol, but Inez grabbed his T-shirt to stop him. No need for an innocent nerd to get hurt in the fray.

"Run!" she said to Ralph.

She pointed at the back door, which stood propped open by the body of the gunned-down skinhead. Rain blew inside, mixing with the spilled blood.

"Come with me!" Ralph said.

Instead, they both stood frozen, watching the race for the pistol. Lucky crawled as fast as he could, but Daniel Delgado, still on his feet, was faster. He reached Lucky just as Lucky reached the gun. Delgado whacked his knee against the side of Lucky's head and sent him sprawling.

Delgado snatched up the pistol and turned to face them. He kept his injured arm against his chest as he ordered Lucky to get up. Inez took some small satisfaction in the fact that she'd hurt him with her clipboard. He backed away a couple of steps to stay out of Lucky's reach as the redhead woozily got to his feet.

"Over there," Delgado said, gesturing with the pistol. Lucky stumbled toward Inez and Ralph, who stood over Jewel, who still sat on floor, shivering, her knees clutched to her chest.

Once they were clumped together, facing Delgado, he gave

them his friendliest business smile and said, "Time to die."

He pointed the pistol at Ralph, who blinked and cringed, then at Lucky, who seemed too dizzy to register the danger.

Behind him, Freddie Garcia said, "Come on, boss. That's enough."

Delgado ignored him, now pointing the gun at Jewel's face. Tears sprang from her eyes, which seemed to delight him.

When he aimed the pistol at Inez, she drew herself up to her full height and lifted her chin at him, daring him, the way José Villa had. That seemed to make up Delgado's mind. He pointed the pistol at her chest.

She watched, fascinated, as his finger tightened on the trigger. Inez thinking: *I'm going to see my own death, coming right at me*. She wanted to close her eyes against the expected flash, but she felt mesmerized by the gun.

Delgado jerked and went stiff all over, but he didn't pull the trigger. The barrel of the pistol dipped toward the floor as his arm fell limply to his side.

His dark eyes were open wide, but they looked blank, and Inez was sure he wasn't seeing anything as he dropped to his knees. A shiny cleaver jutted from the back of his head, dark blood oozing around the blade. He fell forward, face-down on the floor, the cleaver buried in his salt-and-pepper hair.

Jewel screamed.

So did Lucky.

Ralph made a strange gurgling noise, then bent at the waist and upchucked a quart of beige puke all over his own sneakers.

Inez ignored them all. She stared at Freddie Garcia, who stood behind his fallen employer. He seemed thunderstruck, his eyes glazed with shock. An assortment of other cleavers and butcher knives were arrayed on the table beside him, but he made no move toward them.

He'd done enough.

Chapter 67

Ralph Rolfe, already bent over for vomiting, was closest to the pistol, which was still gripped in Daniel Delgado's hand. Coughing and spitting and trying very hard not to look in the direction of that bloody cleaver, Ralph plucked the gun loose and stood up. The small gun felt surprisingly heavy in his hand as he pointed it at Freddie Garcia.

"Don't move."

Ralph wished he could've come up with something better, the way superheroes always have the perfect wisecrack as they're foiling a villain. But it was hard to come up with something clever on the spot.

Garcia seemed shocked by what he'd done. Ralph kept the gun pointed his way as he told the others to call the cops. His voice cracked only a little.

"Good job, Ralph," Lucky said. "You, uh, you want me to hold that gun?"

"I've got it. This guy's not going anywhere."

Lucky shrugged, but he kept looking over his shoulder at Ralph as he helped Jewel to her feet. Her face was streaked by mascara, but she seemed uninjured. Turning away from the sight of the dead men, she pulled a pink phone from her hip pocket and dialed 911.

Inez checked Daniel Delgado and José Villa for any sign of life before she went over to the skinhead at the door and bent to check his neck for a pulse. She apparently found none, because she shook her head as she returned to Ralph's side.

"You could've shut the door," Ralph said. "The rain's coming in."

"The police will want everything left just as it is," Lucky said. He stood with his arms around Jewel, comforting her while she talked with the 911 operator.

"This is a crime scene now," Inez said.

Ralph nodded. He found that he agreed with everything Inez

said. He wondered if that made them soulmates or something.

"Three people have been killed," Jewel said into the phone. "At the *El Matador* butcher shop on Isleta."

They all watched her while she listened, nodding.

"We're not in immediate danger," Jewel said. "The shooter is dead. But a bald guy with a knife may still be outside."

Ralph had all but forgotten about the skinhead who escaped. He kept the gun pointed at Freddie Garcia as he swiveled his head, checking the door and the windows. No sign of the man with the knife.

In the distance, a police siren howled. Sounded like it was coming their way.

Garcia jerked all over, as if he'd suddenly come back into himself. He blinked rapidly, and Ralph thought for a second that he was going to have a seizure. But Garcia managed to focus his eyes on them.

"Let me walk away," he croaked. "Before the cops get here. I'll just go. You'll never see me again."

Inez shook her head. Ralph hesitated only a moment before joining her.

"We'll wait for the cops," he said. "Let them sort it out."

Garcia frowned.

"I'm sorry I ever got mixed up with Daniel Delgado," he said. "The son of bitch is dead, and he's still taking me down with him."

"We'll tell the police you saved the rest of us," Inez said. "It was self-defense. You'll get off. Eventually."

Garcia shook his head, as if that weren't good enough. He looked around the butcher shop. Ralph noticed the way his gaze kept going to the open back door and the rainy night beyond.

"Don't move," Ralph said again. This time, his voice quavered. This time, he wasn't sure it would work.

Chapter 68

Lucky Flanagan wasn't happy about dealing with the police, but he supposed there was no other way. Not with three homicides to report.

He also wasn't happy that Ralph was holding the gun. Not that he didn't trust Ralph, but his friend lived in a fantasy world much of the time. And he'd probably never fired a real gun in his life.

Most of all, Lucky was unhappy about the way Freddie Garcia was edging toward the back door. Taking little sideways steps, like the rest of them wouldn't notice he was headed for the exit.

"Don't move," Ralph said. Third time now. Lucky thought it sounded weaker each time.

Freddie Garcia must've thought so, too, because he suddenly sprinted for the back door, his cowboy boots clumping on the concrete floor.

"Stop!" Ralph shouted.

But Garcia didn't stop. He was almost to the back door when Ralph lifted the pistol and fired a shot into the ceiling. Everyone else froze at the crack of the gunshot, but Garcia didn't even pause.

He was running full-tilt when his boots hit the puddle of rainwater spreading inside the back door. The slick-soled boots shot into the air, as if they were trying to fly off into the night.

Garcia fell backward, too fast to catch himself. The first thing to hit the concrete floor was the back of his head.

Thump!

They all winced in sympathy, and Jewel said, "Ooh!"

Freddie Garcia didn't hear it. He was out cold.

Lucky started toward him, just to make sure, but the rain-slick windows suddenly filled with flashing red lights as two police cars screamed into the parking lot.

"Hey, Ralph," Lucky shouted over the whooping sirens.

"You might want to put that gun on the floor."

Ralph looked at the gun in his hand like he'd forgotten it was there.

"Oh, yeah." He bent and set the pistol on the floor by his feet. "That's a good idea."

"Also," Lucky suggested, "everybody put your hands on your heads."

Inez scoffed. "We didn't do anything wrong."

"The cops don't know that yet. You don't want to be an accident."

Sure enough, the uniformed officers came through the back door with weapons drawn, ready to shoot anybody who twitched. The only ones they found still standing – Lucky and Jewel, Inez and Ralph – stood paired together, their hands on their heads, as the police swarmed into the shop.

Chapter 69

Tino Barreras was glad when he drove out from under the rainstorm. He'd put up the ragtop on the Jeep earlier, but it was leaky and cold raindrops kept finding their way to his skin. He shivered in his wet clothes.

One spot produced plenty of heat, though. The hole in the back of his left thigh – where he'd caught a bullet as he spun away from the door of the butcher shop – burned with a surprising ferocity. His other scrapes and bruises paled in comparison to the hot bite of the bullet.

He had a greasy old towel folded under the wound to soak up the blood, but that was the only treatment he'd bothered to attempt. Once he reached Ciudad Juarez, he could get fixed up by a doctor he knew. Tino thought he wouldn't bleed to death before then.

He was fortunate that it hadn't been worse. He could have easily taken a bullet in the back or in the head. That asshole in the suit had sprayed them with gunshots.

Tears sprang to Tino's eyes as he thought about the bullet hitting his brother's face. Tito might've survived the first two bullet wounds, but that third one spelled death.

Grief washed over Tino. His brother, his only family, was gone. Forever.

He swiped at his eyes with the back of his hand. He was traveling at 80 mph on Interstate 25, headed south. He couldn't afford to be blinded by tears. His grieving would have to wait until after he crossed the Rio Grande.

An image came to his mind: He and Tito when they were kids, eight and nine, swimming in the muddy water of the river, shrieking and laughing and dunking the smaller children. They'd been inseparable their whole lives.

Tino blinked away more tears.

Ah, poor Tito. Always so angry, so quick to react, so quick to kill. He'd succeeded with the old man, that was certain. That knife throw had been a perfect shot to the heart.

Knives and muscle should've been enough to take care of this job. The brothers hadn't expected guns. They hadn't been warned that these Americans, these *bologna smugglers*, might be willing to kill.

For that he blamed Marco Rivera. If Marco had given them a better idea of what to expect, they could've waited until a better time, when they could've caught José Villa alone. But they'd had no warning. They'd plunged out of the rainstorm and into a hail of bullets.

Tino adjusted the folded towel under his thigh. His hand came away red with blood, and he wiped it on his sopping jeans.

He could make it. Just a few hours of driving, and he'd put himself in the care of Dr. Romero. The old doctor had patched him up before. Tino trusted him. Romero could numb the wound and dig out the bullet. Stitch it up to stop the bleeding. It didn't have to be perfect. It only needed to hold up long enough for Tino to accomplish the urgent business of avenging his brother's death.

Soon as he could walk, he'd steal through the night to a particular mansion on the western outskirts of Juarez and find a way inside. He could see himself tiptoeing through the big house while the staff slept, going down the long hallway to the bedroom where Marco Rivera slept on satin sheets.

Tino didn't know what the future held for him, how he'd survive without his brother. But he knew one thing for certain: Marco Rivera must die.

Chapter 70

It was dawn on Sunday by the time the police told Lucky Flanagan he was free to go. By then, he'd convinced himself that he was doomed to prison, that he'd never see the outside world again. So when Detective Stan Ravell, the ferret-faced cop who'd badgered him with questions for hours, told him he could take off, Lucky couldn't quite believe his ears.

"I'm not going to jail?" he blurted.

Ravell frowned at him, as if reconsidering, and Lucky once again wished he'd learn to keep his mouth shut.

"You probably *should* go to jail," the detective said. "You were the catalyst in this thing."

"The what?"

"You started it."

"No, no," Lucky said. "Daniel Delgado and Freddie Garcia started it. I was just there for the finish."

"You smuggled that Rojo into the country."

"They convinced me it was no big deal. Freddie said no one ever went to jail over bologna."

Another frown.

"I'm afraid he was right. It's a federal crime, but I couldn't interest the feds when I called them. I was told no judge wanted that headline."

"Can you blame them?"

Ravell shook his head. "We're playing down the bologna angle with the press ourselves. It just seems so *stupid* that three people died for so little."

Lucky couldn't argue with that.

"Delgado got carried away," he said. "He thought he could build an empire."

"Man, this bologna must be something special."

"It's okay," Lucky said. "But I'll never eat it again. Last time I saw Rojo, it was coming up rather than going down."

"So you said."

Ravell put his hand on the doorknob of the interview room, ready to release Lucky, but he paused once more.

"I guess you know," he said, "the only reason the whole lot of you aren't being held on charges is that your stories agree so exactly. Every one of you said the same damned thing happened in that butcher shop."

"The police got there so fast," Lucky said, "we didn't have a chance to consider any kind of story. We were stuck with the truth."

"And the truth shall set you free," Ravell said, opening the door onto a fluorescent-lit corridor.

Lucky's knees were weak with relief, but he managed to walk through that door.

Chapter 71

Jewel Flanagan was relieved when the elevator doors opened in the lobby of police headquarters and Lucky strolled out. She'd been sitting on a hard bench for the past hour, waiting for him to give her a ride home.

He spotted her right away and strode across the marble-tiled lobby. She stood to meet him, and they embraced for a full minute before either said a word.

"It's over," Lucky said finally. "Let's get you home."

She leaned back to look up into his lumpy, bruised face. "You're not under arrest?"

Lucky shook his head. "Apparently, none of us are."

"Even Freddie Garcia?"

"Hospitalized with a severe concussion, but the cops said he probably won't be charged with anything. I told them he saved our lives."

"I told them the same thing."

Lucky looked over his shoulder at the uniformed cops sitting at the lobby's security desk.

"Let's get out of here."

They went out into the early-morning chill. The clouds were gone, and a pink aura glowed behind the rugged silhouette of the Sandia Mountains. Not for the first time since she'd left home yesterday, Jewel wished she'd worn different clothes. She hadn't known she'd be gone all night, of course, but long pants would've been nice. Running shoes instead of her stupid sandals.

Lucky put his arm around her chilled shoulders as they walked along the sidewalk to where they'd left the Mustang. Once they were inside the car, he cranked up the engine and fiddled with the dashboard dials to get the heater going.

Jewel yawned, then said, "Long night."

"You said it. How many times did the cops make you tell them what happened?"

"Three," she said. "They asked a lot of other questions, too, but it seemed like they already knew the answers."

"I think they talked to your friend Inez first. She laid it out for them, and the rest of us just confirmed what she said."

"I'm glad we had her on our side."

Lucky nodded. He pulled away from the curb, headed toward the freeway.

"Did you see her after we got downtown?"

"She left with Ralph an hour ago," Jewel said. "She said she was giving him a ride home. She offered to take me home, too, but I wanted to wait for you."

"It figures that I'd be the last one the police cut loose."

"You had a lot to tell them," she said. "You're a hero."

The car swerved for a second, as if she'd swatted Lucky with the word.

"Hardly. I put us all in danger."

"You didn't make us barge into that butcher shop," she said. "Once we *were* in there, you kept trying to take control of the situation. Trying to save us."

"Not really—"

"Crawling across the floor after that gun the way you did, on your hands and knees? That was heroic."

"I didn't get the gun."

"No, but you *tried.* And when Daniel pointed that pistol at me, you stepped in front of me, ready to take the bullet yourself. That was a brave decision."

"It was more like a reflex."

"Still. Very brave."

Hardly any traffic at such an early hour, and Lucky steered them up onto the freeway, zipping along.

"I guess I should say I'm sorry," Jewel said.

"For what?"

"For Daniel. I shouldn't have been seeing him. He got you mixed up in all this because of me."

"I got myself mixed up in it," Lucky said. "It looked like easy money, especially the last trip. But I guess I'll never get paid that two thousand now."

"You're still alive. That's more than Villa can say. Or Daniel Delgado."

She shuddered at the memory of the cleaver buried in the back of Daniel's lovely head. If only he'd been as beautiful on the inside as he'd been on the outside.

"Anyway," Lucky said, "no apologies necessary. I'm just glad it's over."

She reached across and rested her arm on his shoulder, her hand on the back of his neck. Lucky's breath seemed to catch at the contact, but he said nothing more. Probably afraid to spoil the moment. She knew exactly how he felt.

Within minutes, they pulled into her driveway. Lucky turned off the headlights so they wouldn't shine in Scarlett's bedroom window.

"She'll be up soon anyway," Jewel said. "And I get to hear from my mother about how I was out all night, and what an irresponsible mom I am."

"Oh, that's right," Lucky said, making a face. "Rayola's in there."

"Don't worry. She's probably asleep."

"Rayola never sleeps."

She lifted her hand off his neck and gave him a playful cuff on the back of the head.

"Ow. No whacking the hero."

Jewel cupped the back of his head in her hand and pulled him close for a kiss. A really nice one. Soft. Warm. Gentle.

When they came up for air, Jewel said, "Oh, my."

Lucky smiled, cradling her in his arms.

"I'd invite you in," she said, "but—"

"Rayola."

"Right. Call me later. Maybe you can come by. Scarlett would love to see you."

"Will do." He leaned in for another kiss, but just a peck this time. "I'll watch you to the door."

Jewel climbed out into the chill and hurried to the front stoop. She turned and waved at Lucky before she went inside.

Chapter 72

When Lucky got home, he found Ralph was still up, sitting cross-legged on the sofa, eating cereal out of a red ceramic bowl. A red box of Cap'n Crunch sat open on the coffee table next to a mostly-empty jug of milk.

"Hungry?" Lucky said.

"Not anymore. Grab a bowl and help yourself."

"I can't eat that sugary cereal. It makes my teeth feel furry."

Ralph ran his tongue around his teeth while Lucky slumped onto the sofa next to him.

"No fur."

"Good," Lucky said.

Ralph pointed his spoon at the muted television. "I'm waiting for the early morning news. They mentioned us in the headlines a little while ago."

"Us?"

"Well, they said three people were killed in the South Valley in a 'business dispute.' Guess that's what the cops are calling it."

Lucky thought there was much more to it than that, but it definitely had been a business dispute, so nobody was exactly lying.

"They didn't name any names?"

"Not so far. Like I said, I'm waiting."

Lucky braced himself. The last thing he wanted was to be mentioned on TV in the same breath as "Mexican bologna." A man can live down a lot of humiliations, but that's the sort of thing that would stick.

"I'm kinda hoping they'll mention Inez," Ralph said. "It would be good for her career."

Lucky cocked an eyebrow at him.

"Since when are you interested in her career?"

Ralph's round face flushed.

"She gave me a ride home. We were talking. There's a lot more to her than you get at first glance."

"Like what?"

"Like she has two cats. Named Boo and Hiss. Isn't that adorable?"

"You're allergic to cats."

"And she's a vegetarian."

"I've seen you eat two Quarter Pounders without coming up for air."

"Maybe we don't have a lot in common," Ralph said. "But she gave me her phone number."

"Like, her business number?"

"Her personal number. I asked her for it and she wrote it down for me."

"You dog, you!"

"I know, right? I'm gonna call her, too. Later. After she's had time to recover."

"Good plan."

They stared at silent commercials flickering on the TV for a minute, then Lucky said, "What about you? You're all recovered? You seem to have your appetite back."

"I threw up everything I'd eaten for the past week," Ralph said. "I had to refuel. But, yeah, I'm doing okay."

"Not every day you see somebody get a cleaver in the head."

Ralph shrugged and shoveled another spoonful into his mouth. *Crunch, crunch, crunch.* Sounded like he was eating gravel.

"I guess Delgado got what he deserved," Lucky said. "He was ready to shoot us all."

"And that other guy, with the tattoos and the knife?" Ralph said. "Hard to feel sorry for him."

"Too bad about Señor Villa, though," Lucky said. "I liked that old coot. I mean, he was a total pain in the ass. But he didn't deserve to die that way."

Ralph nodded, still crunching away.

"I drove him all the way up here just to get him killed," Lucky said. "If he'd stayed home, he would've been fine."

Ralph said something about how it wasn't Lucky's fault, but

Lucky wasn't listening. He'd suddenly remembered something, and it made him bounce to his feet.

"What?" Ralph said. "Is there a spider?"

"His bags."

"What?"

"Señor Villa's luggage. It's still in my trunk."

"The cops didn't confiscate it?"

"I never thought to mention it to them."

"Hmm," Ralph said. "I guess it's your luggage now. Finders keepers and all that."

"I'm not gonna drive it to Juarez and return it to his family, that's for damned sure. I'm done with Mexico."

"Maybe there's something valuable in those bags."

"Let's find out."

Ralph set down his bowl and they went out to the Mustang, which was parked at the curb. Lucky unlocked the trunk and they heaved out the two heavy suitcases. Each carrying a bag, they puffed back into the house.

The bags weren't locked, and they quickly sorted through the old man's clothes and shoes.

"I like these clothes," Ralph said. "This could be my new look."

"They're too small for you. Also, if you suddenly show up wearing guayabera shirts, that'll make people ask questions. I don't want the cops to think we were holding out on them."

"But we were."

"Not on purpose."

Lucky checked a pocket inside the lid of the suitcase he was searching, and his hand found a deck of what felt like paper. His heart hammered as he pulled it out.

Money. Banded stacks of crisp fifty-dollar bills.

"Holy currency, Batman!" Ralph exclaimed. "How much is there?"

Lucky thumbed through the money, quickly counting.

"Looks like five thousand dollars."

"Wow. Señor Villa's retirement money."

"More like his traveling money," Lucky said. "But he's not going to be needing it."

He held the money up to his face and sniffed its sweet scent. It smelled like the answer to all his problems.

Ralph beamed at him.

"Must be your lucky day."

Made in the USA
San Bernardino, CA
23 July 2019